"A charming and very romantic story with ....
The ending puts a perfect cap on the story. I look forward to reading more books in this series to see what happens to some of my favorite supporting characters."

—Fresh Fiction

"Ah, l'amour. I adored this story and the wonderful hero and heroine, who shed all their inhibitions and fears in order to go on the most powerful journey they ever embarked on ... falling in love."

—Smexy Books

"An exciting and sweet historical love story. It has everything that I look for in a good fairy-tale retelling while also tying back to Bradley's earlier books. I am really excited to see more of this series, particularly because of the out-of-control but still entertaining Worthington family."

—Feminist Fairy Tale Reviews

"A laugh-out-loud-funny novel from Celeste Bradley, the third in the Wicked Worthingtons series. Lighthearted but with a few profound moments, it is filled with deception, misunderstanding, exaggeration, cross-dressing, and mistaken identity."

—Harlequin Junkie

Sleepless in Staffordshire

The Haven Holiday Series

Book 1

New York Times Bestselling Author

CELESTE BRADLEY

For Darbi Gill

Friend. Collaborator. Inspiration.
Best. Woman. Ever.

Acknowledgments

I must acknowledge several people for their help in creating *Sleepless in Staffordshire*.

First of all, the writer and director of the film *Sleepless in Seattle*, the incomparable Nora Ephron. Her classic holiday film inspired me to write *Sleepless in Staffordshire* in tribute to a wonderful woman who gave us all so much joy.

I must also thank my wonderful team here at CelesteBradley.com. Charlie Fitch, Darbi Gill, and Geneva Craven Schult, you deserve exotic world travel and spontaneous tea parties!.

Chapter 1

LORD MATTHIAS WATERFORD entered his fine country manor of Havensbeck in county Staffordshire, removed his hat and was promptly greeted by his butler, Jasper. The stout manservant looked dignified as usual in his dark blue livery.

Jasper bowed. "How was your ride, my lord?"

"Cold." Matthias shrugged out of his snow-dusted greatcoat and unwound his woolen scarf. Something caught his eye as he looked up. "Jasper, what is that hideous growth that is even now strangling my banister?"

Jasper wasn't the slightest bit near-sighted, being no older than Matthias's own thirty-two years. Yet he squinted up at the stair railing as if barely able to see to what his master referred. "Oh, that? That is a garland, my lord. A braided strand of winter greenery used to impart a sense of the season."

"Yes, I know what a garland is. Why is a garland allowed to infest my house?"

Jasper beamed at Matthias innocently. "Some people consider them very becoming decorations, my lord."

"Some people may, but not I. Take it down."

"Absolutely. Hideous thing. I shall banish it at once, my lord." The butler bowed so obsequiously low that Matthias could see the top of his ginger-haired head. Sarcasm, in his own house.

Matthias handed his black leather riding gloves to Jasper with an admonishing glare. Then he turned toward his study and the bottle of brandy that awaited him there.

Garlands. Blast it! Christmas just kept coming, every year, again and again, no matter how fast he rode or how far he traveled. So he retreated to this place, Havensbeck, deep in the Staffordshire valley, where the icy cold kept everyone indoors and the heavy snow muffled the sounds of their celebrations. And he still walked in on blasted garlands.

"My lord?"

Matthias sighed and turned to face his most faithful and trusted and annoying retainer. "Out with it, Jasper."

"The Haven assembly rooms are under repair, my lord. Recall that storm last October? The roof leaked most abominably."

"I don't believe a word of it."

Jasper nodded solemnly. "It is quite true, my lord. Mildew everywhere. The blue velvet chair cushions are positively green with stuff growing on them."

"And yet you drape my house with green growing stuff?"

"That's different, my lord." Jasper's tone was starchy. "That's *traditional.*"

Matthias sighed. "Mildew, eh?"

"It is most unrefined, my lord. The ladies will never sit down all night. You will be forced to dance with every single one, at least three times. That is, you would if you still danced."

Pity tinged the butler's voice. Matthias flinched from it, parting his lips to reprimand Jasper. However, those black days of shouting at his devoted servants were long past. "Inform whomever is arranging this event that I will buy new chairs for the hall."

Jasper blinked. "Ah. Yes. That is most generous, of course, my lord. But with only three weeks until Christmas?"

"Ah, you were hoping I would volunteer the manor for the celebrations?"

"Oh, it isn't I, my lord. It's the staff, you see. I'm simply the elected spokesperson." Jasper spread his hands in an apologetic gesture. "I'm fully against it, myself. I loathe people. I despise celebrations. So messy. Dreadful nuisance, guests. If it were up to me, my lord, I would keep the house dark and cold and serve only dry toast and brandy for the next three weeks, just as you prefer. Now, *that's* my sort of Christmas."

Irony, from his own butler. Matthias grunted as he turned away. "Just top off the brandy, Jasper. The dry toast is all yours this evening."

MATTHIAS LEANED BACK in his fireside chair and cupped his snifter in both hands. His study remained quite satisfactorily dark, but it wasn't cold. Jasper would never allow that. A cheery flame traced blue and gold over the coals in the fireplace. From his high-backed chair, Matthias watched it numbly until its merry dance seemed to mock his misery. He closed his eyes against its optimistic flare.

Another Christmas. Another year without Marianna, without his jolly little Simon, without his family. No happy singing of carols, no giddy hiding of gifts, just this bloody great echoing house and another snowy anniversary of that horrible fiery night.

His eyes opened and his gaze slid to the blotter on his desk. Jasper had left out a stack of foolscap and a filled inkwell. Next to the blotter stood a washed, empty wine bottle and a cork at the ready.

Matthias looked away. He didn't know why he bothered. The letters never helped. The entire process was maudlin and unwise and useless. If anyone but Jasper ever learned of it, they would certainly think him mad.

So why did the next moment find him seated at his desk, sharpening a quill? Why did his fingertips grasp the pen, dip it into the ready ink and begin to write?

My dearest Simon,

He wouldn't write to Marianna this time. But a man could pen a letter to his own son, could he not?

The snow is falling on the lawn and I think of you chortling away as your mama tried to show you how to make a snow angel. She moved your little arms and legs and you thought she meant to tickle you. And when she lifted you into her arms and pointed at what you made together, you clapped your hands and shouted "Doggie!" That's when she began to call them snow doggies instead and we made them all over the lawn for you to see the next morning when you awoke.

The coals had gone to gray ash and the house was silent by the time he finished the letter. The pages, when rolled, scarcely fit through the neck of the bottle.

"You are a man of few words, my love," she had told him once with a little laugh in her voice, "but when you take up a pen, you write volumes!

"Only about you," Matthias whispered now. "Only about him."

He corked the bottle tightly and stood, weaving just slightly. He'd been at the desk so long the brandy had nearly worn off, or it would have, if he'd taken the toast. He would have an aching head on him in the morning for his carelessness.

No matter. His step was steady as he left the study and the house. It wasn't a far walk to the stone bridge over the river. His woolen surcoat and weskit would keep him warm enough, even in the snowfall.

The clouds held a glow, for the village was still alight with lanterns and the first round of celebrations. The people of Haven loved a fête, that was for certain. Marianna had adored throwing parties for them all. From baptisms to weddings, she had turned her considerable imagination to pleasing his people. Matthias had always held their respect, but it was Marianna they had loved.

And Simon.

His chest hurt. The hollow pain of loss and helpless fury that smoldered in his heart burned with a special, piercing ache as Christmas Eve approached every year.

The manor had long been repaired. Looking back at it now, no sign remained of the fire damage that had burned the heart right out of its master. Tonight, as the snow fell so peacefully and silently, muffling the faint fiddle music coming from the village, one would think that nothing bad could ever happen in a place so beautiful.

One would be wrong.

Marianna had loved the river. It was known as the River Churnet, a name so old no one remembered what it meant any longer. "Mundane," she had stated, and renamed it the River Celadon and declared it chock full of naiads or dryads or whatever spirits haunted running water. Even now, in the harshest of winters, the swift running water had refused to freeze entirely, leaving a rushing stream down the center of the encroaching ice on both banks.

Matthias leaned his elbows on the sturdy stone railing of the bridge and pressed the freezing glass bottle to his flushed forehead. It was a silly thing to do, writing these letters.

"Stupid. Useless." He held the bottle to his cheek and squeezed his eyes closed. "I love you both. I miss you. Merry Christmas."

And he let the bottle fall into the hissing, rushing water yet again.

Chapter 2

B ERNIE GOODRICH WRAPPED one fist in the back of her brother's thick winter jacket and with the other held tight to the leafless branch over her head. Beneath them, the ice-edged water of the River Churnet swirled gray and white.

"Just a bit more."

"I haven't any more, Simon. Do you want to take a dousing in the ice water and cause Aunt Sarah to carry on about you taking a chill? She'll boil you alive in the tub until you're the color of a cooked lobster!"

"Got it!" Eight-year-old Simon held the bottle aloft like a trophy, brandishing it in triumph.

Bernie pulled him back to the bank with a mighty heave. "Heavens, you're growing. I won't be able to do that for much longer." She set him on his feet and then brushed her fallen hair back into her knitted hat so she could better examine their prize.

"It's a different label than last time," Simon pointed out. "Look, there's a waterwheel on this one."

Bernie tilted her head. "I think it's one of those Dutch inventions. A windmill." She held the greenish-brown bottle to the wintry gray daylight and tried to peer through it. "This one looks chock full of paper!"

"Bernadette Goodrich! What on earth are you doing on the riverbank on such a terrible day?"

Bernie tucked the bottle away into the folds of her skirt as she straightened. "Nothing, Aunt Sarah!" She looked up the bank.

Her aunt gazed down at her from the path above the Churnet, her work-worn fists plunked onto her angular hips. Her brow held the permanent furrows of confusion that Bernie and Simon seemed to inspire in their childless aunt and uncle.

"Are we late for something?" Simon whispered as they clambered up the bank. The grassy slope was covered in a thick fall of snow. They left a trail of footprints, one set small and the other not much larger, in the pristine bank.

It was a good question. "I don't think so, but perhaps?"

It seemed to Bernie that she was usually in the wrong for one thing or another. Tardiness was her usual sin, although according to Aunt Sarah she was also accomplished in Laggardliness and Inattention. In the six years since she and Simon had been sent away from the epidemic that had taken their parents, they had lived in the vicarage of Green Dell and had done their best to adapt. Simon had only been two years of age, so the crumbling house and poor village was all he knew. Bernie, on the other hand, had been fourteen, old enough to recall every moment of another life.

A life very different from this one. "Let's see. We fed the chickens, filled the coal scuttles and turned down the beds."

"I fluffed the pillows!"

"And a fine job you did of it, too." Bernie counted off on the fingers of her woolen gloves. "Chickens, coal, beds, wood-box, and the dough is rising."

"We didn't dust the parlor!"

"Oh, Christmas Bells on a Stick!" Bernie swore. It was Wednesday and the village Ladies League met in the vicarage parlor every week. "Scurry home and get the cloths from the linen basket. I'll put the bread in the oven and meet you in the parlor. Go on! Run!"

Simon bounced ahead of her. If her aunt wasn't lurking watchfully about, Bernie would pick up her skirts and race him home. But the prospect of a lecture on decorum along with the usual one on duty made her head ache just a little bit.

She didn't mean to be a slackard. It wasn't that she minded the constant work, for Aunt Sarah was thrice as industrious herself. None of the chores she'd been set were terribly arduous, at least not now that she was fully grown. It was just that there were so bloody many of them!

And now she'd said bloody in her head, which had to count as some sort of sin. Bernie sighed. It was so easy to sin, living at the vicarage. When Mama and Papa were alive, she'd hardly seemed to sin at all!

The paper-stuffed wine bottle tucked deep into her coat pocket banged against her knee at every step. It was the first one they'd seen this year! Excitement simmered within her, fighting with the frustration that threatened to boil over.

With the Ladies' League gathering at the vicarage today, she and Simon wouldn't have a moment to examine their find until bedtime!

Christmas Bells!

THE DAYS ARE too quiet without you and your mother. The nights are as silent as death itself. Sometimes I must snap my fingers at my ears to be sure I can still hear anything at all. Where is your shriek of glee? Where is your mother's laugh? Did you take them with you onward or are they lost forever?

A POOR VILLAGE meant a poor vicar, if he were an honest fellow. Uncle Isaiah gave everything to his people and they gave back what little they could. Summers were better, when Bernie could fish and pick berries and the hens laid well.

Now, in the winter, bellies were never quite full. The vicarage creaked in the night, and the windows weren't tight enough, and coal was too dear to keep the fire going all night long. Nonetheless, Bernie and Simon had learned to tolerate the chill and darkness to stay up late at night. Aunt Sarah believed in "early to bed, early to rise" and "early birds get the worm" and that keeping late hours made one susceptible to Satan's minions, or was it Satan's mischief? To be certain, Bernie was a terrible listener.

However, fear held no sway over two young people with a yen for a bit of freedom.

Aunt Sarah and Uncle Isaiah had been abed for hours, and Bernie and Simon were sprawled on their bellies on the braided rug in their shared bedchamber, with seventeen letters spread out before them, a single hoarded candle-stub brightening the center of the assortment of stained and wrinkled pages like a spotlight on a stage.

Four of the letters were from the first Christmas after the dam had been built. The next year had brought five, all during the three weeks before Christmas. Then there had been four every year until this one.

Simon touched the corner of today's find. "He sounds different now."

Bernie tilted her head. "How so?" She'd noticed it as well, but she wanted to hear Simon's thoughts. He had a way of looking at things, of seeing the heart of the matter.

"His handwriting is better." Simon pursed his lips. "I think he didn't drink so much brandy this time."

Bernie would have liked to keep such knowledge from his young mind, but there was no keeping anything from Simon's sharp awareness. He was clever, like Papa. But not so serious. Bernie had made sure of that, remembering how to play and laugh herself, fighting through her own grief, just so she didn't have to see the bewildered gravity in his child's eyes anymore.

"Mama would say he is finding his feet." She spoke of their parents easily, had made herself do so when she'd realized that if she did not give them to Simon, no one would.

"Or he ran out of liquor," Simon said, his tone matter-of-fact.

"Or Jasper made extra toast!" She was rewarded by Simon's snicker.

The man who wrote to his lost wife and child didn't mention other names very often, but Bernie and Simon were very fond of the passage from two years past where he had written, "*Jasper despairs of me in these dark times. He would feed me quail in aspic, cake and puddings, filling my hollow spirit with food and pointless celebrations. I take my revenge upon him by refusing anything but dry toast with my brandy. It is petty, but I enjoy it in a small, black-hearted way.*"

Bernie thought Jasper must be a manservant. Simon stoutly maintained that Jasper was the mystery man's best friend. Bernie privately wondered if the letter writer had any friends. If he did, would he spend hours every winter writing to people who were gone?

She'd tried it once, after she'd found the first letters. She'd written to her mother, telling her all about how Simon was growing, and said the cleverest things, and how cold and bare the vicarage was, and how Bernie longed for something more from Aunt Sarah, who worked so hard on other's behalf but never laughed.

When she was done, she felt a bit lighter, but Mama and Papa would never read those words, and Aunt Sarah might, if they were left lying about. Bernie realized that her sixteen-year-old opinions might hurt her aunt, so she tossed the letter into the fire and then stoically endured a scolding for wasting precious paper when Aunt Sarah found the scraps in the coals.

She never wrote another letter. But then, she still had Simon, and her aunt and uncle. *He* only had Jasper.

Looking down, she saw that Simon had fallen asleep, his head pillowed on one skinny arm, his other thumb dangerously close to his mouth. "Just keeping it to hand," she whispered to him with a smile, recalling their father's wry estimation of the practice.

Before she lifted him into the trundle by her own bed, she picked up the latest letter and read it through again.

You thought the snow was magical. So did your mother. So did I. Now it is only cold and wet. But at least, when it lies heavy, it keeps the world at bay.

Beautiful words, yet so sad. Who was this man?

THE HOUSE RESOUNDED with silence. Matthias wandered through the large rooms, his footsteps echoing through the luxurious drawing room with its dark fireplace and through the grand dining room where only a single candle still lighting the room reflected from the many crystals in the chandeliers.

He liked it quiet, of course he did. He was always telling Jasper that. Then Jasper would try to get him to go out, or have guests or make calls. In turn, Matthias refused, avoided and generally disregarded his butler's urgings.

Yet tonight the silence fell stifling. If not for his own steps and the slight creaking of the floors as he was walked, he would've doubted his own hearing. So still.

Some of the staff were likely in the village, enjoying the celebrations. Jasper was generous that way, especially since there was so little occupation with only the master at home. The house could probably do with less staff, but how could Matthias let his people go? Marianna had chosen them, or brought them with her, and even grown a few right here in Haven. They were Marianna's people as much as his.

So he paid them all and he paid them well, and in return they tried to fill their days keeping the manor in gleaming order, ready to host royalty. All for a master who never invited guests, rarely ate dinner, and only infrequently rode his horse.

They could move on. Of course, none of them did. Matthias could feel their loyalty like the heat of a kitchen hearth fire, yet distantly, as if he felt it through the glass panes of sorrow that surrounded him.

It was a big house, and could sustain a large family and all their relations. A few times he had entertained the notion of letting it out, of leasing it to some large boisterous family that would fill the house with the sound of children running, and voices in the dining room, and music in the music room.

Then where would he go, if not here? Another place would not carry the memories of Marianna and Simon. Another place would be strange and sterile and new, at least to him. He would be required to pay attention, and learn new things, and remember which drawer held the buttons and which held the shoehorn.

He didn't want to pay attention. He didn't want to be focused and alert and aware of the present moment. What was the present moment to him? It held no Marianna and Simon.

It held no one at all.

BERNIE MIGHT NOT care for the never-ending labor of keeping house, but she appreciated the ritual of visits to the ill and infirm. It was Aunt Sarah's duty as the vicar's wife, but Sarah hadn't the patience for tending the sick and had gladly handed the responsibility over to Bernie.

Bernie's father had been a physician and her mother, his brilliant assistant. Bernie recalled riding in Papa's carriage from one fine house to the next, sometimes helping with tasks like bandaging a slight wound, sometimes banished to a parlor to wait while a lady gave birth.

Going on rounds in the tiny village of Green Dell reminded Bernie of those times and the way her father's calm manner and her mother's soothing voice would ease the worry in someone's eyes. In her own fashion, she tried to do them proud. Simon tagged along, for he was always happy to talk to anyone who couldn't escape his chatter.

"Mrs. Small, do you know about a little boy who died?"

In the cramped but sturdy cottage of the village's foremost matriarch, Bernie kept her hands busy plumping the old woman's pillows as she cast her little brother a warning glare.

Simon blinked innocently, his large green eyes shining with angelic sweetness. The little beast. Bernie's hands smoothed the complicated quilt and smiled at Mrs. Small. "Don't mind Simon. He has a bee in his bonnet."

Mrs. Small smiled indulgently at Simon. "No, he's a dear, he is! What little boy, pet?"

Simon had chosen his mark carefully. Mrs. Small adored gossip.

Simon approached the bed, reaching out to touch the quilt with a single chubby finger, every inch the wistful waif. Bernie sent him a cynical glance. He had no shame at all.

"I heard a story, Mrs. Small," he said breathlessly. "A sad story, about a little boy and his name was Simon, just like me!"

Bernie fought not to roll her eyes. Her brother was entirely able to speak in perfect sentences, not this babyish blurting. Still, she hesitated to scold him now. Mrs. Small had been hoarding information for every one of her seventy-eight years. If she hadn't badly twisted her ankle on the icy lane a few days earlier before, she would probably be out collecting some more tidbits at this very moment. If anyone had knowledge about the mysterious Marianna and the man who mourned her, it would be Ellie Small.

Besides, Bernie could always scold Simon later.

Mrs. Small fidgeted with her covers, eager to chat. "My goodness! What a story, little one! There have been a lot of boys named Simon over the years. Do you know when this happened?"

Bernie went to the table by the fire to pour Mrs. Small a fresh cup of tea. Not that she was trying to lubricate the old woman's memory, or anything so self-serving. Simply being thoughtful, that was all.

"Probably not more than a few winters ago," she said over her shoulder, keeping her tone slightly indifferent. Simon could play the inquisitive waif, but she could not pull off such a feat without seeming strange and desperate. "I think it happened around this time of year."

"Coming on Christmas? Goodness, that would be a sad tale! Wait a moment. Did you say this happened here in the village?"

"I don't think so. Upriver, perhaps." Bernie gave a little dismissive smile as she served Mrs. Small her tea, cup on the saucer, handle turned just so, presented with both hands, exactly the way Mama had taught her in another time, another world. Then she turned a mild glare on her brother. "It isn't important. Just some old story he heard. I'm sure you wouldn't recall a thing about it."

Shame on her, throwing down the gossip gauntlet like that and challenging Mrs. Small's knowledge of local history!

She was a terrible person. She secretly vowed to come back tomorrow and scrub Ellie's kitchen floor to make up for it.

Her guilt appeased by such a penance, Bernie took a chair from the table by the fire and brought it to the bedside. Simon snuggled closer to the coverlet and gazed up at Mrs. Small with wide-eyed wonder.

Now fully invested in proving her infallibility, Mrs. Small sipped her tea and squinted at the far wall, visibly combing through decades of collected tittle-tattle.

"Simon," she mused aloud. "There was Simon Cooper, the boy that fell out of the hayloft and never woke from it. Of course, he was near sixteen." She glanced at her listeners, checking for confirmation.

Simon shook his head. "No, this one was littler than me."

"Ah. How sad." More tea. More scrutiny of the distant wallpaper. "There was young Simon Morton. He had the burst appendix. He was a wee lad, no more than six or seven."

Bernie leaned closer. "Upriver?"

Mrs. Small tapped her fingers on the rim of her teacup. "No, no, downriver. In Beekerton, or thereabouts."

"But there was also the lady." Simon pressed close, visibly willing Mrs. Small's extensive memory to do its magic. "His mother died and he died, too."

Mrs. Small blinked. "Together? Oh heavens. Well, that would be that poor woman upriver, then, wouldn't it? What was her name?"

Bernie sat with her fists clenched in her lap, unable to deny her own need to know any longer. "Mm?"

"Marianna!" Mrs. Small burst out. "That's it! Oh my, what a tragic tale. Her and her little boy dying in that fire! Why, the entire county was aghast! But that had to be seven years back."

A year before she and Simon had arrived at the vicarage. That explained why they'd not heard about it at the time. And if anyone had ever mentioned it to Bernie in the time soon after her own loss, she wouldn't have noticed past her own pain.

But now?

"Seven years?" Marianna's husband still mourned his wife and son with desperate intensity.

Bernie fought the urge to clutch her own Simon close in that moment. She didn't know what it meant to lose a spouse, but if she ever lost her dear little beast, she thought it quite possible that she would die on the spot.

Or expire slowly and alone, piece by piece crumbling under the pain, dissolving to nothing over all the years of her life.

Just like him.

She'd fixated on the letters as if they were a story, an escape from her humdrum life, a romantic tale in some book Aunt Sarah would disapprove of. Now, she pressed her palm to her middle in response to the jolt of true compassion she felt for the man who wrote them. *You poor soul.*

Suddenly ashamed of herself, she stood and brushed briskly at her skirts. "Well, Simon, it's time to leave Mrs. Small to rest."

"Lady Marianna and little Lord Simon," sighed Mrs. Small. "We all mourned, the whole valley. Poor, poor Lord Matthias!"

His name is Matthias.

And then, swiftly on the heels of that thought came another.

Lord? He's a lord?

Bernie swallowed hard. Not simply a gentleman but one of the nobility. And just like that, some little candle of hope, some secret dream she'd not even known she had, some fantasy was snuffed out by a chill draft of reality. She was of decent birth. Her mother was a lady, her father a gentleman, a respected man of medicine. She'd been born to a gentler life, a life of tea rituals and calling cards and lace on her underthings, but a titled match was still as far out of her reach as if she truly was just a poor vicar's daughter.

However, Simon was agog. "Lord Matthias? What's he lord of?"

"Why, he's the lord of Havensbeck Manor, he is! It's one of the oldest houses in the county." Mrs. Small announced proudly. "Some say that's what our river used to be called, back in Cromwell's time. Haven's Beck."

Simon looked at Bernie, his eyes wide, practically jiggling with excitement. "Beck, that's another word for river, right? It's him, it has to be him! And he's a lord, Bernie! He's a lord and he needs a wife!"

Bernie clapped a firm hand right over Simon's mouth and smiled fixedly at Mrs. Small. "If there's nothing else you need, we'd best be on our way!"

She managed to keep Simon's exuberance suppressed until she'd gathered up her basket of jars of bone broth and dried herbs and shoved him out onto the walk outside of Mrs. Small's front door.

Then he turned on her, all coy sweetness stripped away. He folded his skinny arms and glared at her. "I found him. I found Lord Matthias! And you don't even care!"

She looked away, tugging her skirts out of the snow and picking her way down the lane. "I care. It's good to have it settled and done."

Simon ran in front of her and blocked her way with a challenging glare. "You need to write him back! You need to write a letter right now!"

Bernie drew back. "I need to do no such thing!" Except that she had thought about it, if she ever found out his identity. She would write a letter and he would write back to her and someday they would meet.

Her baby brother, her darling, the child who adored her above all others, stared at her with scorn. "Coward."

She lifted her chin. "You wouldn't understand," she said loftily, against the sting of his disapproval. "After all, you're just a little boy." She picked up her skirts and whisked around him. It was time to finish her visits to the ailing and get back to the vicarage, where she belonged.

Chapter 3

"Y OUR POST, MY lord."

Matthias glanced at the silver salver piled with envelopes, presented by Jasper as if it held the scrolls of Alexander the Great. Matthias looked away. "You know what to do with the invitations, Jasper."

Jasper didn't sigh, or grimace, but Matthias could feel his butler's disappointment. "My lord, there are several fine families within a half day's ride from Havensbeck who would be honored to have you at their table."

Fine families with suitable daughters. Matthias could hear the unsaid words vibrate through the room. He ignored them, even as he ignored the pile of post. Finally, Jasper fished out two letters from the heap of rich, creamy paper carrying blobs of wax with monograms and family crests pressed thereupon. These two missives, refreshingly free of ornate seals, came from a firm that oversaw his investments in London.

He set the letters aside to read later.

Jasper still stood by the desk, the salver in one hand, an opened letter in the other. Matthias looked up to see an odd expression on his butler's face. Not that Jasper would ever go so far as to smile, but there was something strange about him. "What are you reading?"

Instead of answering directly, Jasper began to read aloud.

"Dear my lord sir,

I am writing to you because you need a wife. I am needing a husband, so this is excellent news."

Oh, bother. Most women were more subtle, but every once in a while Matthias received a more, ahem, forthright offer from a person of the female persuasion.

"No more, please. God, I hate those letters."

Jasper gazed at the letter. "I rather like this one." He continued reading.

"I am comely and I have a nice smile. You will be happy to know that my gowns are getting tight in the bosom."

Matthias twitched irritably. Bosoms were the last thing on his mind. Although he recalled being very fond of them, once.

"I am very cheerful and I like to laugh. When the cow got out and ran through the garden with Aunt Sarah's bloomers on her horns, I laughed so hard that I had to sit down. I by chance sat upon the--"

Matthias looked up to see Jasper watching him.

"Do you wish me to stop, my lord?"

Matthias drew back. Damn it, he'd actually begun to be interested in that drivel! "Indeed I do. I believe I said as much."

Jasper nodded a bow as he flipped the letter back into its folds and tucked it into the stack of invitations. Matthias noticed that the paper of that peculiar offer was not fine, nor creamy, nor held an imprinted seal. In fact, it looked almost like butcher's paper, addressed in a smudged, blocky print.

No, thank you. He drew the line at women who could not use a quill properly.

Jasper took himself off at last and Matthias turned back to his reports of bushels and barrels. An image drifted across his mind's eye, a cow galloping clumsily about, a crown of lacy underthings flying like a banner from its blunted horns.

He didn't laugh, not quite.

I wonder what she sat on?

OUTSIDE HIS LORDSHIP'S study, Jasper paused in the hallway to finish the letter.

"I by chance sat upon the sundial. I had to use a cushion at the dinner table for nearly a week.

If you would like to have a wife who can cook and bake and clean, I would like to have a husband who is a lord. I know a lot about tea and I am not afraid of dogs. Also I am a very good fisherman."

"Very good fisherman" was crossed out in heavy, blotted strokes. After it was written, *"lady who fishes very well."*

As he was alone in the hallway, Jasper allowed himself a real smile.

The closing clearly spelled out *"Miss Bernadette Goodrich, the*

Vicarage of Green Dell, County Staffordshire" in the same blocky letters. There was no signature.

Jasper folded the letter once more and tapped it thoughtfully against the edge of the salver. Downriver. As head butler, Jasper took his duties very seriously. His lordship depended on him to take care of household matters, to see to the grounds and to keep things in good repair. When something in his purview was broken, Jasper had great power of discretion to fix it.

Fix it he would. Yes, indeed.

BERNIE STARED AT her aunt and uncle across the breakfast table. "A holiday? In Haven?"

Beside her, Simon wriggled in his chair. She felt his pointy elbow in her side.

"Upriver!" he whispered loudly.

Bernie absently caught the offending elbow in a gentle but uncompromising grip as she waited for Uncle Isaiah to confirm Aunt Sarah's announcement.

He smiled benignly at her. "Wouldn't you like that, Bernadette? It was young John Barton who extended the invitation. He's vicar there now. He has asked us all to join him for the holiday celebrations at the manor of the lord of Havensbeck."

"*Havensbeck!*" Simon squeaked.

Bernie felt her belly flip. Visit *his* manor? Eat at *his* table?

Aunt Sarah nodded. "You remember John, don't you, Bernie? He was studying with Isaiah when you first arrived here. Such a likable young man."

Bernie blinked. Aunt Sarah, who refrained from being judgmental with all her might, for that would be a sin, also abstained from dropping praise. Ever.

She looked down at her polished plate. She'd eaten every scrap of her toast spread with drippings and her meager allotment of bacon, except for the piece she'd slipped to Simon while her aunt served her uncle.

Of course, she recalled John Barton. He'd been tall and thin and fervent at eighteen, all big hands and stumbling feet and burning belief in his mission to bring salvation to the straying flocks of the world, whether they wished it or not. At fourteen, she had found him admirable but not terribly approachable.

Bernie was all for salvation, but she was of the opinion that, if let be, the flocks would likely exercise a little self-restraint of their own. Most people simply wanted enough coal on their hearth and enough food for their children. She much preferred Uncle Isaiah's kindly, uplifting sermons. He made people remember that being good was good for everyone, that kindness begat kindness and generosity of spirit could be infectious.

Mr. Barton may have mellowed, she reminded herself. He would be in his mid-twenties and had finished his studies and his curacy under another vicar before being ordained. He would have seen more of the world, and the world was a great teacher. She was prepared to give him the benefit of the doubt, friend of the family that he was.

There was no other reason she was eager to go upriver to Haven. None whatsoever.

ONCE PERMISSION HAD been granted to host the holiday festivities in the manor proper, the entire staff of Havensbeck had lost their minds.

At least, that was how it seemed to Matthias. Every room he passed, every hall he traversed contained some madness of the housekeeping kind. Apparently, entertaining a few hundred people for a single meal required that every square inch of Havensbeck be unfolded, aired, swept, polished, turned inside out and upside down. Chaos reigned and Matthias found himself helpless against the tide of revolution.

"Pardon me, my lord, but I'll be needin' to dust that." Before he'd fully planted his arse in a chair.

"If you're finished with your tea, my lord, I'll just be clearing it away." Before he'd taken a single sip.

"Apologies, m'lord, but you can't go in just now. The maids are waxing that floor."

"It's my study! There won't be any guests visiting my study!" Grumbling was met with cheerfully insincere regret, and he found himself shuffled off into another room, and yet another, until Jasper finally suggested that his lordship had some overdue business with the solicitor in the village and wasn't it a fine day for a ride?

Matthias, knowing full well he was being ousted, took up the excuse to leave and allowed himself to be stuffed into his greatcoat. In mere minutes, he found himself thrust from his own house. His stallion, Perseus, stood saddled and ready in the center of the snowy drive.

The day *was* brilliantly clear, with blue skies and sunlight shimmering on the heavy blanket of snow. The drifts on either side were high, but the lane to the village had been compacted neatly by the many carts that had delivered to Havensbeck in the last few days. Grousing to himself about the cost of all those supplies could not keep the cheering glory of the bright winter day from affecting him. By the time he reached the village common, he found his mood somewhat less gloomy.

Blast it, he hated it when Jasper was right!

BERNIE SQUIRMED IN her seat. The long carriage ride from Green Dell to Haven had been wearing for Simon, and even more so for the adults accompanying him. He was a sweet boy and always eager to please, but six slow hours was difficult for an active child.

Immediately upon arrival at the inn in Haven, before the bags were even fully down, Bernie whisked her brother out of sight of her weary uncle and visibly frazzled aunt.

A good run around the village, that's what they needed. To be honest, Bernie was no more used to sitting still for that long. In the course of her duties, she had become accustomed to constant action and long walks.

Aunt Sarah waved them off gratefully as she entered the inn with her husband. Uncle Isaiah leaned heavily on his walking stick, ashen with fatigue. Bernie felt bad about leaving them until she noted that the innkeeper's wife had taken an instant motherly interest in her newest guests.

Running would be improper. Walking so briskly that it might as well be a running pace was merely efficient. And if she danced into a skipping step occasionally, it was only to keep up with Simon, who fled the carriage and the inn as if they were on fire.

"Come along, Bernie! I want to *see*!"

See what, she could not imagine. Anything at all, she supposed, other than Green Dell. A different baker, a different smithy, even a different tree would be a significant novelty over the village he'd not left once since the age of two.

Bernie remembered London. Mostly her memories of the city itself were a blur of sooty buildings and crowded walks, but she'd been to Regent's Park many times and once she had accompanied her parents to Brighton and seen the sea. Yet even she embraced the giddy feeling of visiting a new village. New faces, new shop fronts, new signs above them.

Haven was more prosperous than Green Dell, that much was obvious at once. The women looked less work-worn, the men more satisfied with their lot.

When they passed the vicarage, the residence attached to the Haven church, Bernie looked curiously through the iron gate. There were piles of cut lumber and stacks of stones waiting next to the small stable, covered with canvas tarpaulins and ready to make the improvements to the living quarters of Haven's new vicar. Even before the proposed changes, she could see that solid stone house was larger and finer than their own.

What a difference it made, having one's landowner in residence. The farms around Green Dell belonged to an elderly count whom Bernie had never seen. Beleaguered by generations of debt, the man could not sell the estate, nor would anyone let it, not in the condition it stood now. So the old hall sat empty and crumbling and there was no one to turn to when a field flooded or a sickness swept through the sheep herds.

When she turned away from the vicarage gate, Bernie realized that she'd lost Simon. Again.

Excellent. No one could chastise her for running now.

MR. ESTON WERMER, solicitor, accountant, investment manager and Havensbeck's foremost defender against the drift of entropy, was a narrow fellow with hands beginning to twist with age and a back bending under the weight of it. His most distinguishing feature was a full head of shocking white hair. His office was on the story above the bookshop with a view of the village square.

"My lord! Why did not you send for me to come to Havensbeck? It is not fitting for you to clamber up my stairs!"

Matthias didn't bother to remind Wermer that he climbed more stairs at Havensbeck Manor before breakfast than comprised the short flight above the bookseller's.

Wermer took Matthias's greatcoat and gloves, hat and scarf. It didn't help much, for the room was oppressively warm. Wermer must have noticed Matthias's deepening flush, for he moved to the large window and pushed one half of the glass outward on its hinges. Matthias nodded in gratitude and promptly took up a position near the fresh air.

In his turn, Wermer tugged his own scarf more snugly around his neck. "My apologies, my lord. I cannot suffer the chill the way I used to."

Matthias waved a hand, already losing interest in the temperature. "Tell me, Wermer. What have you discovered about that farm tenant? Was I correct in my guess that Fulton is withholding illegally?"

Wermer cleared his throat, clearly uncomfortable. "No, my lord. On closer questioning, I discovered that the farm had recently come under the management of the original tenant's sons. According to one rather severely annoyed wife, the three young men have squabbled so extensively over one particularly excellent field that they neglected all the others. Poor old Fulton."

Matthias nodded encouragingly, but all he could think was, *three sons? A wealth greater than any land.*

"I took the liberty of giving all three fellows a sound scolding and promised them that they would lose their tenancy if they did not see to their plantings more conscientiously this coming spring!"

"Yes, yes, very good. Your efforts are most appreciated. And the old farmer, Fulton. What happened to him? I had not heard of any deaths in the village."

"No, my lord. Old Fulton resides by the fire, too frail for farming. Do not worry over him, my lord. His daughters-in-law dote upon him fiercely."

"Siiiimonnn!"

Marianna?

Matthias flinched. Wermer gazed at him curiously. No ghostly presence invaded the room. *Am I losing my sanity?*

"Simon, where are you?"

No, the source of the call lay outside the room, out in the square. Matthias found himself at the window, looking for the caller, his heart pounding. Which was a bit insane, now that he thought about it. After all, Simon was a common name and the woman only sounded a little like Marianna.

Yet he could not keep his eyes from searching for a dark-haired, slender lady who favored blue silk and smiled as if she held a secret. Behind him, Wermer said something. Matthias ignored him.

A boy ran across his field of vision. He was a skinny lad of less than ten years, with a too-large knitted hat tugged down over his ears and booted feet skidding on the snow-packed cobbles.

The child waved a stick like a wooden sword in his mitten paw. He slewed to a stop to give challenge to a cart horse tied outside the dry goods shop.

"*En garde*, you despicable dragon!"

The cart horse slid a contemptuous glance at the brave knight, then went back to nosing the small pile of hay that had been dropped at his post.

"Simon, that horse works for his living. He has no time to play with you."

Matthias looked up quickly at that musical voice, but the young woman walking across the square was nothing at all like Marianna. He could not see her face well in the shadows of her bonnet, but her figure was fuller and her bulky canvas coat fit her ill. She looked like a farmer's daughter come to the village to gawk over the lengths of ribbon in the milliner's shop.

Still, she had a very nice voice.

Young Simon turned to her. "Bernie, do horses get bored?"

To Matthias's surprise, the young woman stopped and tilted her head as she considered the harnessed animal with apparent seriousness. "I would imagine that were I a horse, I should rather like to be bored. Horses are skittish and fearful sometimes, so for one to be bored, he would need to feel so very safe for so very long that he had actually forgotten what it was like to be afraid."

An interesting thought. Matthias frowned at the horse.

The boy eyed the oblivious animal with new curiosity. "And *then* they would get bored?"

Matthias found himself waiting for her answer. The girl had to be sister, not mother, for the child had called her by a family nickname.

She nodded decisively. "Yes, then they would get bored."

Now that he'd established that the girl with the nice voice was nothing like his Marianna, he found himself fascinated by the child. His own Simon would be a bit older than this lad. Would his little man have been so awkward, with oversized, scuffling feet and odd, curious questions?

Matthias tried to recall what he had been like at that age. The door of his recollection opened stiffly, creaking with disuse. For so long, his memory had swirled ceaselessly around a few precious years and one awful night. It took an effort to reach back through the continuum of his own existence to recall the lad he'd been at ten.

Quiet. A little bookish. Mad about stories of faraway lands and strange peoples. Good on horseback, but yes, constantly tripping over his suddenly large feet.

And a good seventeen years away from meeting a girl with a teasing smile and eyes like blue glass before a candle flame. It startled Matthias to think of his life before Marianna, before Simon, before that awful Christmas Eve.

I had twenty-four years before. Happy years, full of friends and adventure, with not a dull moment or second of wistful melancholy. For a single, fierce instant he longed with all that was left of his soul for that other Matthias, that whole, unbroken young self.

Then shame doused him, like an icicle dripping down the back of his neck. He straightened, pulling his hands back from the sill and turning sharply away. He would have to abandon his wife and son, to leave them to their end, unremembered and unmourned, to be that man again.

Besides, he wasn't sure he even recalled how.

Chapter 4

"M Y HEAVENS, WHAT a *sociable* place this is!" Aunt Sarah's tone was not as approving as one might suppose. She picked at the sumptuous tea tray as if more interested in finding a hidden drawback than in eating anything.

The village of Haven was so prosperous that Bernie could understand her aunt's wistful envy. It would be much less strenuous to be a vicar's wife in Haven than in Green Dell. Poor Aunt Sarah.

Bernie herself was utterly charmed by the bright-eyed welcome everyone seemed to have for the vicar's party from downriver. The innkeeper and his wife were deeply solicitous of the weary older couple. Aunt Sarah wasn't one to let others do for her, but even she was gratified by the way their hosts fluttered about Uncle Isaiah.

After Bernie had confirmed that her aunt and uncle were safely snugged into a private dining room with steaming cups of tea in their hands and hot bricks beneath their feet, she took Simon to their rooms to get them all unpacked.

She found that they'd been given the best rooms in the inn, ones with thick featherbeds, heaping wood bins and wide windows that looked out over the pretty village and the fields beyond.

"I can see the vicarage from here!" Simon, up on tiptoe, pressed his little nose against the diamond-shaped panes of glass.

"You can likely see Green Dell from there," commented Bernie drily, although she had to secretly admit to being rather impressed herself. As John Barton's guests, they were being enfolded into the arms of the village as if they'd finally come home.

There was a tap on the door and two maids entered. A matched set of blondes, they were rosy-cheeked and pert with importance as they briskly shook out Bernie's limited wardrobe, hanging her gowns and tucking her underthings discreetly into a chest. In no time at all, far faster than Bernie could have accomplished it, the trunks were unpacked and carted away to be stored during their stay.

Simon didn't notice, of course. When he turned to see the room set to order, with his own spare set of pants dangling from a hook in the wardrobe and his treasured wooden horse set neatly by his bedside, he seemed to take the transformation in stride. Bernie regarded him with fond exasperation.

Born to be served. Perhaps it was a peculiarly male thing.

Bernie tried to give the maids the farthing she kept in her pocket, but they giggled and rolled their eyes at her.

"Aw, miss, that'd be too wrong of us. Honored guests, that's what you are!"

The other girl nodded, her black curls bouncing. "That's right, miss!"

Simon yelped. "Bernie, I see him! I think it's John Barton. Is it? Is it him, Bernie?"

Simon was very eager to see John. At the age of two, he'd followed the young man about like a baby duck. Bernie doubted that he truly remembered John well, but Simon knew that his beloved toy horse had been carved by John and had decided that John was a kindred soul, a brother of the spirit, torn away by cruel fate.

In short, a hero.

Bernie certainly hoped Mr. Barton would not disappoint her little brother. She scurried to the window and pressed her own nose to the glass, peering through the frost-etched pane into the bright courtyard.

She saw a tall shadow pass beneath them and she wondered if she recognized some aspect of bearing. "I think we ought to go downstairs and see."

Simon pounded out of the bedchamber before Bernie could so much as dip her head down to the vanity mirror to check her appearance. Not bad. A little windblown, for certain, and her gown needed pressing after that carriage ride, but her jaunt about the village with Simon had put becoming roses into her cheeks. Not that she cared one whit how she appeared.

Still, it might be John Barton. Or it might not.

MATTHIAS HAD LEFT his mount in the sturdy hands of the innkeeper's stableboy, for he'd thought his business with Wermer might take a while. Now he stood at Perseus's head in the doorway of the horse-warmed stable and fiddled with the bridle. As he re-buckled the cheek pieces, and straightened the throatlatch, which didn't need straightening, for no Havensbeck groom would send his lordship out in slapdash trappings, Matthias gazed pensively down the curving main street of Haven.

Who was she? He didn't think she was local. She was well spoken, clearly not a farmer's wife. Perhaps a nearby squire had taken a bride? If he could've seen her hands without the gloves he might've spotted whether or not she wore a ring.

Not that it mattered that she was single or wed. He simply wasn't accustomed to strangers in his village. Having someone new visit would be occasion to comment, surely. In fact, he was surprised that Jasper had not said a word about newcomers. Matthias wished he had, for then he would've already known who the girl was and therefore could promptly forget her.

It was probably only the boy who'd caught his curiosity. A little boy named Simon? Of course his attention was riveted. It was only natural that he be curious about a child with his son's name. Was it not?

Strangers usually stayed at the inn. And he was already here.

MATTHIAS STEPPED OVER THE THRESHOLD of the Haven's Rest Inn and blinked against the dimness after the bright afternoon outside. Once again he found himself unbearably warm.

Did he keep Havensbeck so cold that he couldn't bear a normal interior any longer? How grim.

A pretty little maid rushed out to the antechamber with a smile, which promptly disappeared as she gave a yelp of surprise at seeing him there. Her eyes were enormous as she put both hands over her mouth. She bobbed repeatedly as she backed away from him and scuttled back down the hallway.

Now he was frightening girls. Perfect.

A clatter of shoes brought the innkeeper, red-faced and puffing as he barreled into the foyer with his hands spread wide. "Your lordship! Oh, heavens!" He struggled for breath. "Welcome! How may I serve you today?"

Matthias gazed blankly at him. *I came in pursuit of a woman.* That wouldn't sound bizarre at all. Instead, he lifted his chin and fell back upon his social stature to gaze down at the man impassively.

He found that if he did this when he was at a loss for words, people usually filled in the blanks themselves.

The innkeeper paled, then reddened, then clasped his hands in front of him and grimaced painfully. "The maid is just shy, my lord. She's a good girl, she is. She meant no disrespect. She was that surprised to see you here, is all."

Blast it. Now everyone would think him a harsh fellow, berating a young woman for her moment of panic. He tried to ease the sternness of his expression. Sadly, he seemed to be out of practice. "I saw no fault in your maid, good sir. Your own swift arrival was most gracious." He bowed his head slightly. "I thank you for your prompt attention."

The man calmed at that. His face resumed something of its usual cheerful expression.

Matthias could not remember his name. He known it once, of course he had. The fellow had taken over this inn from his father, and probably his father before that. A family in his village for generations and he couldn't remember the blasted man's name.

What had he become?

"I merely stepped in to warm myself for a moment." This was certainly true, as he was sweltering. The inn was stifling, although no one else seemed to mind it. "How is business, Cransby?"

There. He done it. He dragged the man's name out of the murky past. Hadn't he?

The innkeeper hesitated and then licked his lips. "It's Cranston, my lord, but no matter. And business is right smart at the moment, thank you for asking. When the word got out the Christmas ball was going to be at the manor house as of old, folks decided to come from all around the county."

Matthias stared at the fellow blankly. "The Christmas ball, you say, at the manor?"

The man beamed. "It's awfully generous of your lordship to put on a special dinner and all. Oh, the missus is right thrilled, she is. Isn't a woman in town the village who isn't pressing her best dress right now!"

Not a simple village assembly. A ball. With a dinner. At the manor. Matthias held his breath for a long moment.

Jasper was the devil. Jasper must die.

AT THE TOP OF THE stairs leading down to the main rooms of the inn, Bernie paused as Simon pulled his hand from hers.

"I forgot my horse!" Simon dashed back toward their bedchamber. Bernie took a moment to smooth the lace at her neckline and check that her shoes were dry enough to escape notice.

"And have you had much new business due to the upcoming ball?"

The deep voice came from below, from the front hallway at the base of the stairs. The baritone rumble of the masculine tone were nothing like the innkeeper's cheerful tenor, or even Uncle Isaiah's resounding pulpit voice. *Who is that?*

The innkeeper spoke. "Oh, I'd say so for certain, milord."

Milord. It was *him*. Of course it was him. He sounded just as she'd heard him in her thoughts every time she'd read his letters. Bernie's heart began to race and she pressed her palms there as if to capture it and keep it where it belonged. Biting her bottom lip, she slid her foot down a step and bent to peer through the spindles of the railing.

"There's some has come from the remote farms, and there'll be more, I reckon, when the day comes. Folks don't want to be kept to home because of the weather." The innkeeper went on. "And of course, there's the vicar's people what come today."

"John Barton? I wasn't aware that he had family nearby."

Oh, that voice.

Bernie slid down one more step, then another, until she could make out a broad shoulder in a black greatcoat. The rest was blocked by the angle of the stair and by the innkeeper's stout form in his brown jacket. The innkeeper was taller than she was and yet this fellow loomed over him. Oh, if only they would move a step to the right!

"Be not so much relations as they be friends, I'd say," the innkeeper went on. "It's his vicar from downriver, the one that trained him up. He's right chuffed they could come. We're all puttin' out our best foot, like. Fine folks, they are."

His lordship had come to ask about *them*? Uncle Isaiah and Aunt Sarah and Simon and *her*? Suddenly recalling her hoydenish antics in the village, Bernie blushed hotly. He'd seen her gallivanting about with Simon? And in that awful redingote that made her look as shapeless as a bear, too! And Simon in his ill-fitting boots and patched trousers? She deeply regretted the urge that had led her to save her good things for the upcoming special occasion. Oh, what a picture they must've made playing in the snow and foolsing about with the old horse!

She could hardly blame the lord of the hall for coming to the inn to learn more about the odd newcomers disporting themselves so familiarly in his pretty village. Yet, was he so strict a master that the girls did not run and the boys did not fight off imaginary dragons?

"And is it only the elder vicar and his wife?"

The innkeeper burbled on even though Bernie wished to slap her hand over his overactive mouth. "There is the miss and the little boy, come to see good John. I don't know for sure now, so I shouldn't be telling, but if you were to ask me I'd say it is Miss Bernadette Goodrich that John Vicar be so eager to see."

"The vicar's daughter?"

"I believe she be a ward, or a niece, or summat like that, milord."

"Well, I suppose that would be a good match for John."

Heavens, even strangers were all to ready to marry her off!

The innkeeper made an agreeable noise. "She's a pretty thing and sturdy, too, which is a handy thing for a vicar's wife."

Sturdy? Bernie wanted to die.

"And I'm thinkin' John will make a good father to the little lad. It'd be a blessin' all around for the old folks to get Miss Bernadette sorted away and young Simon raised proper."

Sorted away, like a spool of thread in a sewing box. And what was wrong with the way Simon was raised so far?

Bernie hadn't realized that she'd made it all the way down to the landing until his lordship moved slightly sideways and she found herself with a perfect view of his face. She pressed closer to the spindles.

He was not perfect, as she'd imagined. First of all, he was younger, perhaps a bit over thirty, although there was something weary in his expression. His face seemed carved of some fine and valuable stone. He was winter-pale, against dark hair and dark eyes. Were they brown? Or perhaps blue. Shadowed by loss? He wore black, from his greatcoat to his trousers and boots. Even the scarf tossed loosely around his throat was the color of soot.

Yet for all his darkness, he did not appear threatening or even brooding. He seemed *still*. Not the stillness of a tranquil soul, overflowing with contentment. More the stillness of a hooded hawk held by its jesses in a falconer's grip. Confined, not panicked so much as waiting.

Waiting for you? Hardly. He barely knows you exist.

So there he was, standing before her as real and solid as a man could be. Not words on paper. Not a silly schoolgirl dream. A real man.

No, a lord. A heart-stopping, handsome, tragic, lonely lord who waited for a beautiful lady to free him, a princess on a quest sent to unlock his grief-chained heart.

Not her, in her canvas coat and her scuffed walking boots, a penniless burdensome orphan, trailed by her beloved, skinny, snot-nosed little brother.

A scuffling noise brought Bernie out of her avid crouch where she knelt clutching the spindles of the staircase like a naughty child banned from the party below. She straightened, and briskly brushed at her skirts even as she took a breath to make some silly excuse about her odd behavior.

It was only Simon. He also hunkered on the steps above with his entire head thrust between the spindles, ogling the scene below. Bernie grabbed for the back of his jacket and yanked him toward her. His mouth she did manage to clap her hand over.

"Not a word, I shall boil your drawers in poison oak!" she hissed in his ear.

The threat held and he stopped struggling, although he emitted an offended sniff. She would never do such a thing on purpose, of course, but apparently the one accidental incident had made an impression.

In the moment of suppressing Simon's urgency, who apparently intended for her to run downstairs and throw herself into his lordship's arms, the man himself managed to make his farewell to the innkeeper and slip away. Bernie resisted the urge to clatter down the stairs and watch him ride away through one of the windows.

Simon glared at her with his eyes full of the trenchant disappointment that only an eight-year-old could convey. He clearly thought she was a complete idiot, and had allowed an obvious opportunity to pass for some sisterly reason for which he had no patience.

She didn't answer his betrayed gaze, but merely pushed his hair back into place, straightened his collar and motivated him the rest of the way down the stairs with a quick tap on his backside. "Aunt Sarah and Uncle Isaiah are expecting us. Shoo!"

The same goes for you, she commanded her wayward thoughts.

Good heavens, Lord Matthias was delicious!

Chapter 5

M ISS GOODRICH!" JOHN Barton stepped forward eagerly enough to greet her when she reached the dining room where her aunt and uncle had been stowed. He even smiled a little.

Had he always been that handsome? All tall, fair and burly, with eyes as gray and familiar as a misty day? Bernie swallowed back her surprise long enough to dip a little curtsy. "Vicar Barton."

She thought she might have gained a clue as to why the new vicar had been openly embraced by the citizens of Haven!

He held out his hand to her and she gave him hers out of sheer stunned confusion. She'd left her gloves upstairs. His hand was so large and warm it was as if she'd pressed her palm to a fire-warmed hearth stone. She looked down and away, feeling a little strange.

His gaze never left her. "You have grown into a woman. When I saw you last, you put me in mind of a colt, you were so skittish and awkward. Just look at you now!"

There was no need to wonder what he was thinking. The admiration in his eyes was undeniable. Bernie found herself ridiculously flattered. His open regard was a balm to her frayed nerves and self-inflicted humiliation over her hoydenish jaunt through the village.

She stammered out a thank-you, then wrinkled her nose at herself. "I am still a little awkward, I think," she said with a rueful smile. "But your words were far too kind. It is you who have grown into a person of accomplishment and stature." Really, she could only be formal for so long. She squinted up at him. "You're rather like a tree, I think, sir."

Simon giggled from behind her skirts, where he'd hidden when struck by a sudden bout of bashfulness.

John Barton took a knee, right there in the dining room, and peered around Bernie. "Who is that? Did you bring me a pixie to cause me mischief, Vicar Goodrich?"

He frowned, but the mock seriousness did nothing to dim the twinkle in his eyes. "No, I believe it is a giggledom. Or possibly a conflugated narfsplat."

Bernie felt Simon jiggling with glee behind her.

"Narfsplat! Hee-hee!"

Tall, eye-catching and good with shy little boys. He was too good to be true—except that he was true. She knew him. She knew all about him. This outstanding fellow was no stranger to her at all.

He glanced up at her, the smile still tugging at his lips. "I know they are a timid species, those narfsplats, but do you suppose you could introduce me? I've always wanted to meet one."

Bernie introduced Simon, tugging him out from behind her with the strength born of years of practice. Simon, contrary little monster that he was, was immediately distracted by the heaping tray of tea cakes and spiced biscuits.

"Oh, that's all right," John told her when she apologized for her brother's defection. "Eating is important work at that age."

Bernie barely heard him, lost in thought. He seemed like the perfect man.

There must be a catch.

They sat down to a splendid cream tea, very nearly a luncheon. Bernie buttered a roll for her brother and tried to keep her mind on the visit and not on the shadowed gaze of a certain mysterious lord.

Simon wolfed down a manly portion of confections and tea, then gazed longingly at the bright day with his face pressed to yet another window. Bernie shook her head, thinking of all the nose prints he was leaving behind him.

"I want to go out again, Bernie. Please-please-please?"

Bernie glanced at her aunt and uncle. Aunt Sarah was gazing listlessly at the fire and Uncle Isaiah was frankly dozing in his chair. She ought to make sure they made it to their room before they collapsed.

Once again, John Barton came to her rescue. A discreet tug at a bell rope brought back the innkeeper's wife. Mrs. Cranston clapped her hands, conjuring maids who cleared the table in a wink and coaxed Aunt Sarah to her feet.

Roused, Uncle Isaiah waved the younger folks out. "Go on, Bernie dear. Let John show you his fine vicarage."

Bernie squinted at her uncle. She'd met John again, just as she'd promised. There was no reason to push the point! She'd rather go to her room and read through Lord Matthias's letters again, this time knowing his voice and his handsome face. But Simon bounced with enthusiasm so Bernie stifled a sigh and made polite noises about John's graciousness and such, then back upstairs to fetch their coats.

THE VICARAGE WAS not so much under repairs as it was enduring improvements. Fresh paint and a new carpet were apparently not enough for the generous lord of the manor.

John gazed about his new home with wry consternation. "I did tell his lordship this wasn't necessary, you know. I would have been happy with a full coal bin and the odd visit from a housekeeper."

Bernie was peering at the fine marble fireplace in the dining room. This house had a dining room, a breakfast room, a formal drawing room and a snug family parlor. The enlarged kitchens—plural!—had been equipped with multiple stoves, sinks, pumps and larders.

"It does seem rather expansive for a bachelor," she said absently.

John cleared his throat. "Well, I think the intention is that I take a bride at some point."

Bernie went still. She hadn't meant to point the conversation in that direction. Luckily, Bernie was saved from complete stammering gracelessness by Simon's call through the open door.

"Berniiiee! Come see! There's a stable! With a horse in it!"

"Very nice! Really! Must go catch up with Simon!" She practically ran from the house.

What are you running from?

She couldn't explain it, even to herself, but the fact remained that she could only breathe naturally when she stood out in the snow with the sky like a blue bowl over her head.

When John followed her out, she turned to him with a determined smile. "It's far too fine a day to dawdle indoors!"

He kept his pleasant expression, but it took on a faint puzzlement. "It is cold enough to freeze butter outdoors."

She waved a hand in dismissal of the temperature. "Simon and I are entirely used to the cold. Our landlord doesn't believe in full coal bins." That was true enough, so she didn't understand the stricken look in his eyes.

"I fear I have much to do this afternoon," John said reluctantly. "But if you want to see a bit of the valley, you should take the lane toward Havensbeck." He pointed. "I should like to catch up to you and Simon when I'm able."

Bernie looked away. "Yes. Of course. I look forward to it."

She turned away from John and set out to chase her brother down. "Come along, Simon! Don't you want to look around the village a bit more?"

He whirled, skidding in his oversized boots. "I want to see Havensbeck!" Then he took off again. Bernie was close behind, happy to run off the discomfort caused by her oddly intimate moment with John Barton. A tromp in the snow was just the thing.

It wasn't at all that she wanted to see the manor over the river.

Or the man who dwelled within it.

THE WINTER SUN, commonly weak and neglectful, today glinted brilliantly off the fresh snowfall on the Havensbeck fields. Although the light did nothing to melt the snow, and his breath still puffed white as pipe-smoke, the air was still. Even Matthias's great black horse seemed to feel it, slowing his walk until he trudged down the lane toward Havensbeck like a plow horse, eyes lazily half-closed against the bright day.

Matthias allowed it, and even found himself gazing at the clear blue of the sky in some astonishment. Had he ever seen such a vivid day in December? Since he usually spent this month knowing little but the sullen crackle of his study fire and the fierce bite of whisky in his throat, he could honestly say that he had not spent a day like this in many years.

The silence was broken only the fall of Perseus's great round hooves and even those were muffled by the packed snow on the lane. Deep gouges had been cut by cartwheels into the knee-high powder, pressed down again and again by the many deliveries to the manor. The rest of the world lay covered, smoothed and rounded and silenced by the sparkling blanket of white.

Until a flying ball of snow struck Perseus smack in the nose.

Icy granules spattered Matthias's face and he blinked in surprise. Perseus squealed and tightened his haunches. Then the world turned upside down.

Chapter 6

MATTHIAS OPENED HIS eyes to find himself blinded by white. No, not blinded. Buried. He'd landed arse-first in a snow drift. It has closed over him as softly as a velvet fist.

Truly, he'd never taken such a comfortable fall from a horse. He got his feet under him and fought upward. He easily broke free of the soft, powdery pile, but he got a mouthful of snow for his efforts.

As he coughed to clear his air passage, he felt hands grasping his own. They tugged hard. Matthias tried to protest that he was not badly stuck, but it was too late. He tumbled out and down again, this time falling onto warm bundles of soft cloth and bony limbs.

"Oof!" It was a female voice, full of breathless amusement.

Another voice was frankly giggling. A child.

Hurriedly Matthias swiped at the snow sticking to his face with one hand while using the other to scramble backward off someone.

Oh blast. Off the woman he'd landed on with all his weight!

"Are you hurt, miss?" He stood quickly and leaned down to offer her a hand.

She lay on her back in the snow and held up one palm to stay him. "Simon?" she gasped, winded.

Simon. Matthias shook the snow from his vision and peered at the other person in the snow. A pointy, freckled face peered up at him from where the boy sat in the snow with his oversized boots spread wide.

"Your horse," he said with an admiring tone, "is fast."

"He is also somewhat temperamental," Matthias informed the boy.

Simon nodded wisely. "That's what everyone says when they fall off their horses."

"I didn't fall."

An alarming peeping sound began to emanate from the young woman. Matthias frowned at her. She looked nearly terrified, Or possibly confused. Was she afraid of him?

Her entire body started to quiver. Then her wide green eyes clenched shut and tears began to squeeze from between her lids. Matthias drew in a breath to reassure her that his lordly dignity was not permanently damaged.

She gave up the fight and dropped her hands away from a husky, chortling laugh that seemed to take over her entire being. He looked at the boy, but young Simon simply grinned up at him.

The two feral creatures were entirely unashamed of the results of their errant missile. Matthias was considering stalking away in a proper huff when he realized that he wanted to stay to hear more of that infectious laughter. The young woman laughed as unselfconsciously as a child, sitting up and wrapping her arms about her bent knees as she doubled up in spasms of it.

So Matthias stood like a chunk of obsidian in a bubbling stream, letting the sound of it wash over his stolid black-coated presence, the same presence that had left poor Cranston aquiver with unease.

The flow finally began to trickle off. The young woman inhaled a steadying breath and pressed her gloved palms against her midriff, as if she meant to push back the last rising giggle. The gloves were knitted of the same stuff as the boy's flopping mittens. Even from where he stood, he could see flaws in the pattern. She'd knit them for herself and her brother, he would wager. Did she not mind the imperfections? Or was she simply too impatient to rip it out and do it up right?

Matthias would guess the latter. There was something liberated and self-assured about her, despite her plain coat and felted wool bonnet that reminded him of something his mother had worn when working in her precious roses.

He waited as she finished composing herself. She lifted a hand to smooth away the tears coating her cheeks. They were smooth cheeks, young. Yet he had the feeling she was no schoolgirl.

"I do apologize, sir. I am told I am inclined to humor at the most inappropriate times." She took Matthias's hand then and allowed him to pull her to her feet. The girl from the square was not as bulky as she appeared to be, for she came up lightly with a sideways smile.

There was no demure dropping of her eyes, no timidity at all in her frank green gaze. Instead, he saw something that startled him to his core.

Sympathy. And shadows.

He ought to recognize them, having seen them in his own mirror for so many years. This young woman had seen terrible loss, just like he had.

And yet still she laughed.

Matthias felt overcome by a sudden thirst, a yearning for this secret, this arcane knowledge that shone from the open, half-smiling face of this girl like a beacon on a stormy coastline.

Tell me. Show me.

Teach me how to live again.

His legs had already began to flex in preparation for taking a step toward her when she spoke.

"I do hope your horse will be all right."

Matthias caught himself before he did something strange and inappropriate. He'd been working on that, he truly had. He no longer wore his raw pain on the outside, like a skinned beast. He didn't roar at his staff, he didn't smash his possessions and he didn't fall at the feet of strange women and beg to know their deepest secrets.

"And you, too, of course," she continued with belated concern. "I hope you didn't hurt your, ah," her lips twitched again. "Your person."

From her expression of barely suppressed laughter and young Simon's open grin, Matthias surmised that his fall from Perseus had been somehow spectacular. "I must have put on quite a show."

Simon pointed out toward the road. "You flew up!" His mitten-clad hand lifted in illustration, exposing a bony little wrist. "And then you stayed up!" The fingers spread and Matthias pictured himself hanging in the air. "And then you dropped!" The floating hand thumped firmly down onto the palm of the other hand. "Right on your ar -- "

A sisterly boot kicked him in one skinny shin. "Ow." Simon balanced on one leg and rubbed at his offended shinbone as he glared at his sister. "Bernie, I was only going to say 'ar -- "

Matthias shouldn't think of her as Bernie, for they'd not been properly introduced and he didn't wish to bungle his newly regained manners by calling her by her given name, even in his mind, for then he'd only forget and let it fall from his lips.

However, she stuck out her hand like man. "I'm sorry, sir. I'm Bernadette Goodrich and this is my brother, Simon. Our family is visiting Havensbeck's vicar for the holiday." She leaned closer. "Tell me, is the Christmas dinner at the manor as generous as we've heard? I hope so, for I fully intend to make a pig of myself."

"Me, too!" Simon looked for all the world like a starving orphan, with his wide green eyes and pinched features. Matthias could well believe the boy could put away a plate or three come Christmas Day.

Matthias wondered if they had any idea who he was. To all appearances he was just a gentleman in a black coat on a fast horse, not a lord in a glossy carriage with a golden crest emblazoned on the door.

Strangers were a novelty for him. It seemed everywhere he went, people knew him or knew of him, and had heard the tragic tale. He was an object of pity, or alarm, as if loss was contagious, and the rumors of his raging, pain-filled first years of mourning preceded him.

So he simply nodded. "I have not attended for some time, but I have heard the manor staff is exerting themselves immensely."

Simon goggled. "Staff? Like servants? Serving us?"

Miss Goodrich wrapped an affectionate hand around the back of her brother's neck and shook him gently, sisterly and maternal at once. "No, idiot. They are going to toss our dinner into the trough and let us fight for it."

Simon snickered at that. "Snort-snort. You said you'd make a pig of yourself."

Then he turned to Matthias. "I found a badger burrow. Do you want to see?" He pointed back over the wall.

Matthias raised his brows. "Really?" Teaksmith, his gamekeeper, was meticulous about eliminating pests, although he might have let a badger family burrow this in this particular field because alfalfa was not something they were known to eat. Instead, they would likely prey on rabbits and insects, which would benefit the crop.

However, badgers did not interest him nearly as much as did this unusual young woman and her Simon.

His heart flipped sideways at the radiance in her eyes. Light, among the shadows? This young woman had discovered a secret. She'd found the hidden path to the place beyond the pain, a world where the lost were remembered but no longer mourned.

He wanted that, suddenly, so abruptly that he could hardly breathe.

Disloyal. Selfish. He shouldn't want to laugh in the sunlight with this strange young woman while Marianna and Simon could not.

Confused and shaken, he was about to make his goodbyes when a male voice hailed them from down the lane.

John Barton, the new young vicar that Matthias had selected for Haven, strode toward them. His open face was smiling but there was a crease of concern between his brows nonetheless.

Matthias wondered if it was such a strange sight for him to be seen talking to actual people, and decided that it likely was. John bowed slightly. "Lord Matthias! I see you have met Haven's latest visitor, Miss Goodrich."

"And me!" Simon informed the man. "I pulled him out of the snow!"

Miss Goodrich gave her brother a little shove that rocked him sideways a step. "After you smacked his mount in the face with a snowball!"

"That was an accident!" Simon protested weakly. Then he manfully turned to face Matthias. "But it *was* me, your lordship. I'm awful sorry. I was aiming for Bernie, but she ducked and then there you were behind her."

The boy's narrow face was tight with anxiety. Matthias realized that it was because he was frowning down at the child like an angry tyrant. *I am not used to talking to children. I am not used to talking to anyone.*

All the more reason to try.

So he knelt with one knee in the snow to bring himself to Simon's eye level. "Is it customary for you to throw snowballs at ladies, young Simon Goodrich?"

Simon writhed in place. "Nnoooo. But it was just Bernie!"

Matthias continued to gaze at the boy. "Hitting Perseus was an accident. Accidents are easily forgiven. Throwing a snowball at a lady was not an accident. It is not I to whom you should apologize."

Simon slid an astonished look at his sister. "I'm sorry, Bernie. I forgot you were a lady."

She reached out to ruffle his hair. "I'm afraid I forgot as well, beastie. But Lord Matthias is quite right. 'Tis a poor practice, to be sure. I imagine John can find someone your age to bombard with snowballs. Is that not so, John?"

She smiled at the vicar. When John Barton smiled back at Miss Goodrich, there was something in his gaze that made Matthias look away. So, the girl who carried laughter and shadows in her green eyes had already caught the interest of Haven's most eligible bachelor.

Matthias backed away a step. "If you will all excuse me, I must head home." He looked up the lane toward Havensbeck. "At least Perseus ran in the right direction."

The young vicar, who was not actually so very much younger than Matthias, didn't take his eyes from the pretty girl who had suddenly made Matthias notice pretty girls again. "Very well, my lord. I should be getting these two back to the inn."

As always in England, the goodbyes took too long. Matthias abruptly wanted to get away from the three of them and the confusing tangle of curiosity, alarm, envy and longing they caused within him.

When they turned away to head toward Haven, Matthias saw the girl look back over her shoulder at him. Was it his imagination, or did he see a sort of message there? Perhaps a certain absolution of his brusqueness and his poor abilities in society? Understanding, at least. But no pity. Not a bit of it.

We don't pity each other, he thought, *we who have lost. We understand.*

IT WAS FORTUNATE for Bernie that Simon had lost all his shyness in John's presence. Her little brother chattered nonstop as he explained the fascinating encounter with the badger burrow and gave, at length, the details of his lordship's magnificent flight through the air from his horse. Allowing Simon to dominate the conversation left Bernie time to contemplate Lord Matthias in the privacy of her own mind.

Yes, he was tall. Yes, he was dark-haired. But her brief glimpse at the inn, and even her years-long perusal of his letters, had not prepared her for the tilt of his head when he listened or his serious gaze when eye-to-eye with Simon or the way he continuously looked at her and then glanced away as if strangely uncertain about her.

She'd tried to convey her very harmlessness, much as if coaxing a wild thing to her hand to accept a bit of winter corn. Not that his lordship was anything like a squirrel or a deer. He was most definitely powerful and masculine. He was also strangely reticent and, she suspected, a bit broken.

It was decidedly odd to encounter someone who had so much and yet so little. For all his wealth and fine house and even his highly populated staff and village, he seemed very alone. How could that be? All Bernie had in the world were her aunt, her uncle and her little brother, yet she rarely felt lonely. In fact, she felt as if she could scarcely find a second to herself.

Were his people so frightened of his shadow that they shied away from him? The people in the village spoke about the great house with pride and how prosperous and generous the estate was, but said little about the man himself.

So who kept whom at a distance? If it was Lord Matthias himself who was too grand, she'd not seen it. In fact, she felt oddly as if he had almost reached out to her more than once.

It wasn't as if she were terribly special, and she'd certainly given him a most disorderly impression of her. He no doubt thought Simon unruly and ill-behaved and herself plain and dumpy. Simon could behave perfectly well, at least when he not been confined in a carriage all day and then admittedly encouraged to run himself in giddy circles afterward. And perhaps she was no renowned beauty, but she was hardly dumpy at all! It was only this blasted coat!

Anyway, his lordship had not looked at her *that* way. Or not quite. She couldn't put her finger on exactly how he had looked at her.

She, on the other hand, had looked at him very much *that* way. Her breathless excitement at meeting him face-to-face had been passably well covered by her fit of giggles. She shuddered at the impression that must have made! But then she'd reached out and shaken his hand as if they were nothing but two farmers meeting on the lane!

That was too bad of her. It wouldn't do to go thinking she actually knew him! Reading his letters the last several years, private, personal letters from him to his lost wife and child, did not make her his confidante! It made her a prying, sneaky busybody.

Except she hadn't been intentionally sneaky. And the letters had practically arrived at her back doorstep! Had he never considered those bottles might wash up somewhere, and the letters taken out by perfectly innocent people, and read over and over again by the light of a candle in the middle of the night?

She hid her blush from Simon and John by pretending a great interest in the naked branches of the trees merging overhead of the lane, lacing together like bony fingers, while she allowed her thoughts to linger on the feeling of Lord Matthias's large hand wrapping about hers.

John noticed her interest. "They bloom. It's very nice in the spring."

Bernie turned to him, startled. "What? Pardon me, I mean to say?" There she went, making a fool of herself in front of a man again! Not that John counted exactly, old family friend that he was. Young, handsome, undeniably appealing old family friend. Why didn't John's forthright friendly manner and symmetrical features linger in her thoughts the way Lord Matthias's did? Honestly, she'd almost forgotten John walked next to her at all.

Aunt Sarah was right. She was, without a doubt, a master of inattention.

She fixed her gaze on John's handsome, open face and gave him her best bright-eyed attention. "These trees bloom in the spring?"

He laughed at her but not unkindly. "These trees, which are some sort of fruit, do indeed bloom in the spring. I've only been here one spring but when I called upon his lordship this lane was incredibly beautiful and the pink petals began to blow down as I passed. I felt quite poetic trying to think of a way to describe the snowfall of pink fragrance." He gave a self-deprecating laugh.

He'd visited the manor? Well, of course he had. He was the vicar here now. In just a few days she would see it for herself, for the Christmas Ball.

John continued to speak about the sights of Haven in the springtime. Their pace was sedate and the day very still around them.

So why did the world seem to be shifting beneath her feet? Since the moment she'd looked into Lord Matthias's dark, shadowed eyes, she'd felt as though she dangled from a great height, clinging to the merest winter twig, where any moment something fragile might snap and she might fall so far she would not survive.

Chapter 7

T HE JOURNEY BACK to the manor was easily walked in summer. In midwinter, it was not near so pleasant a stroll. By the time Matthias had limped, slipped and slithered his way down the snowy lane in boots never made for walking in snow, his mood had descended to a place between exasperated and bitterly amused.

It seemed there was nothing like a bit of physical discomfort to make a man feel alive. That had to be it. The girl with the candid green gaze seemed destined for another man, a deserving man. It was naught but the embarrassing fall and the discomfiting walk home after the fleeing Perseus that had Matthias's blood running warm through his veins and his thoughts jittering from the satisfaction of horse roasting to the boyish thrill of a pretty girl's attentions.

Jasper met him at the door. "My lord, are you well?" He helped Matthias out of his coat and scarf. "The groom just told me he found Perseus back in his own stall with his saddle still on!"

Devious beast. The stallion's gall tripped Matthias's mood into full amusement. He let out a rusty noise, a husky gasp that might someday grow up into a laugh. The strange utterance made both himself and Jasper blink in surprise.

To cover both his alarm and his strange mood, Matthias turned a glare on to his butler. "Jasper, I am informed that the Havensbeck Christmas Ball is much anticipated in the village. In fact, the entire county of Staffordshire seems to be in quite a twist over my upcoming fête."

Jasper's expression became fixed, although his eyes widened. Matthias imagined that Perseus had felt much the same about that misbehaving snowball.

Jasper swallowed hard. "Er, yes, my lord. The ah, wee village assembly, you mean? Did you not give permission?" Jasper had the decency to trail off before claiming any such thing.

Matthias shook his head. "Give it up, Jasper. It's a full-blown ball by now, whether you intended so or not. I suggest you stock the larder and lay in a fresh supply of coal. And acquire gobs of greenery. That is the fashion now, is it not?"

Jasper smiled widely. "Yes, my lord! Verily so, my lord!" He bobbed several enthused bows as he retreated, carrying Matthias's winter outerwear. "We'll do the manor up proper, you shall see!" he called over his shoulder as he turned away, in an apparent hurry to do dubious things to innocent evergreens.

"Tea, Jasper!" Matthias bellowed to his triumphant butler. "In my study!"

Matthias eased gingerly into his chair in his study, then sighed in relief. Not so bad as he'd expected. Thank Haven for snow banks and fine furniture!

The handsome green leather chair matched another one by the fire, set off nicely by the warm dark wood of the panels on the lower portion of the walls. A carpet of blue and green weave lay over nearly the entire floor, muffling sound and making the study warm. He used to like this room, he recalled, yet despite using it every day, he'd not truly looked at it in years.

Havensbeck had good old Wermer, of course, but Matthias liked to keep his hand in when it came to the tenants. The improvements to the vicarage were coming along, according to the notes. John Barton had been a good choice, although Matthias wasn't sure there was enough work in Haven for a young man of Barton's energy and vitality.

A vision of Miss Goodrich arose. He saw again those vivid green eyes above the rustic mittens clamped over her mouth. Laughing at him.

John Barton was courting her? Matthias fought the tightening of his neck muscles. The notion made sense, and John should certainly marry. A vicar's wife would be good for Haven. She would do much to make up for the lack of a lady of the manor.

But John was a serious fellow and Miss Goodrich clearly loved to laugh.

His twisting thoughts were interrupted by the entrance of Jasper, backing into the room, lugging a vast tray. Matthias looked up sharply.

"Jasper, do you know if our new vicar plans to marry soon?"

Jasper went quite still and thought a moment rather too long on it, in Matthias's opinion.

"Marry? The *vicar*?" Jasper seemed deeply surprised by the notion for some reason.

"Yes. He is squiring a young lady about. The ward of his former teacher, it seems. She is interesting." *Startling. Disquieting. Compelling.* "Rather pretty."

"John Barton the vicar is courting *Vicar Goodrich's niece*?" The crockery clinked on the tray.

Matthias blinked at his butler. "Is that so odd?" Perhaps there was a good reason it would be a bad match? Matthias found himself very interested to hear it, if so.

Jasper shook himself free of his shock. "I wouldn't know. Your tea, my lord." He stepped forward to plunk down a tray as tempting as a child's dream. Minced ham sandwiches, the fresh-baked bread cut in the shapes of stars. Iced tea cakes with precious cardamom and currants. Steaming tea, ready to be poured into a china cup so fine one could almost read through it. There were even two elegant slices of fresh lemon, grown in Spain and held in a locked basket in the Havensbeck root cellar like the pure gold it was.

Matthias stared at the tray. "I am not a schoolboy, Jasper. I did not request cakes, or stars, or gumdrops or spun-sugar jesters with bells on their caps."

"What, my lord?" Jasper looked distracted even in the face of his lordship's bafflement. "Oh, yes. Your ritual fast."

"It's not a ritual!"

Jasper expression turned a little exasperated. "Well, cooks *cook*, my lord. It is what they live for. You keep one of the finest cooks in England on your staff and you expect him to be fulfilled by poached eggs and toast?"

Matthias scowled at him. It wasn't a ritual. It was just a habit. "Just pour the tea! Then get thee gone, wearisome creature."

Jasper dashed from the study, muttering. Matthias couldn't be sure, but it sounded like, "The *vicar*? Oh, no, no, *no*!"

AFTER THE TEA AND SANDWICHES, Matthias did feel a bit clearer as he examined his records.

The rents from the three northernmost farms in the valley had grown scanty. Matthias had decided to try to solve the puzzle without speaking again to Wermer. Low yield could be attributed to many things, and he did not want to make a mistake by criticizing another farmer who had suffered some sort of mishap.

He shuffled through his papers, looking for the weather tallies from the past year. Had it rained too much? Not enough? He honestly had no idea.

The notion shocked him somewhat. As he flipped sheets to one side, he thought back. What about the year before? Had it been a good year or bad? And the year before that?

He hadn't a single notion. It wasn't as though he'd noticed and now the answer escaped him. Shame tingled within him. He'd been a poor master indeed if he could not track his own lands!

Jasper had left the iced cardamom cakes, tucked in next to the sandwiches. Matthias could call him back to take them away, but the damned butler was so bloody annoying these days.

In truth, they were delicious. His cook was most definitely excellent.

Matthias had not hired the man. Marianna had. He had a dim memory of her interviewing dozens of eager applicants, trying so many dishes she'd complained she would never keep her figure if she did not find one soon enough. She'd been such a proud hostess, and her table the talk of London and Staffordshire alike, for she never traveled without the fellow.

She'd been marvelous at everything. Matthias had been unable to believe that Miss Marianna Shepherd had chosen him, over all the barons and earls that had followed her to ball after ball. He was only the son of a younger son, with a comfortable estate but no title. He saw little possibility of his suit against the titled suitors who paid assiduous court with flowery phrases and cheeky innuendo.

Straightforward Marianna had wanted nothing to do with their banter and gossip. "No one ever says anything *real*."

That was the first thing she'd ever said to him. It hadn't even been directly to him. He'd heard her mutter it after dragging her hands from the sweaty grip of some braggart with the dance skills of a baboon. When she'd turned away from the man, she'd found Matthias directly before her. Knowing she'd been overheard, she blushed. Even when awkward, she'd been so bloody stunning.

Matthias had bowed and offered his hand, without saying a word. She'd given him a sideways smile, absolutely aware of what he was doing. He really wasn't much of a conversationalist, but his tutors had made certain that he was an accomplished dancer. He'd swept her into a waltz and danced two numbers through, and never spoke a word.

She'd accepted the gift of his silence and lost herself in the dance, floating blissfully about the floor like an angel with a tiny wicked grin on her lips. When the second song ended, Matthias had to set her free or face social censure for impropriety. But as he left her, he bowed over her hand. "Thank you, Lady Marianna Waterford."

She'd narrowed her eyes at his presumption at planting his name on her own, but the smile still tugged at the corners of her perfect lips. "Lord Matthias Waterford is getting ahead of himself," she said archly. "But time will tell."

They'd been wed the following month, oblivious to anyone in Society who might look askance at their brief courtship. Even the most cynical wag had to admit that their blissful happiness could not be denied.

So very happy, for such a very little while.

The short winter day had faded, and night had fallen in the study, turning the comforting masculine colors to gloomy shadows of themselves. Another day gone, another day closer to the anniversary of that night.

Matthias pushed away his tea and reached for his brandy.

And his quill.

MATTHIAS OPENED HIS eyes, and blinked as the room around him swam into focus. Instead of viewing his richly appointed bedchamber, he found himself looking about his dim, cold study. It must be early if Jasper wasn't yet about. Only the slightest blue light peeked through the large windows facing the garden.

He probably ought to have had a little more tea and a little less brandy. It had been a long time since he had woken at his desk after a night of determined drinking. He thought he'd passed that stage years ago.

Oddly, he did not feel hung-over. In fact, except for the crick in his neck from sleeping in his chair, he felt fine. Glancing to one side he saw his brandy snifter only half emptied and the decanter beside it with one glass gone from its contents.

This was new. It seemed he'd forgotten to get drunk. Yet, spread out on his blotter before him were the pages he had written to Marianna and Simon last night. That much had not changed.

He gathered them up and rolled them tightly, not bothering to read them. No doubt he had said what he always said, that he missed them, and he ached for them, that he had no idea how he was to continue throughout the many years left of his life without them.

As always there was a bottle with the cork ready standing on the side table by his desk, the greenish glass dark in the dim light. Jasper knew. It was Christmastime, after all.

By the time Matthias had shrugged on his surcoat, and buttoned his waistcoat, the light coming in the window had warmed from gray to blue. Picking up the bottle that he had filled with his longing, and capped with his loss, he walked through the silent house and out his own front door into the dawn.

THIS WEEK IN HAVEN was meant to be a time of rest but Bernie could not shake her habit of early rising, much as she would have liked to. Of course, it didn't help that Simon was bouncing on her mattress well before the sun rose.

"Come on! Come on, come on, come on!"

"Shh! You'll rouse the place and then Aunt and Uncle will find something useful for us to do!" Bernie grumbled as she rolled out of bed, for the mattress was soft and thick and the room was warm. However, she herself was eager for another day in Haven.

They were not the first to rise in the inn, but nearly so. The drowsy serving girl waited on their breakfast in a leisurely fashion. Between yawns, she smiled at Bernie and ruffled Simon's hair.

"Be you excited for the feast, miss?"

Bernie swallowed, and hid the thrill she felt at the very thought of the Christmas Ball at Havensbeck Manor. "We are," she replied. "Everyone says it's going to be astonishing."

The girl's grin widened. "Oh, it'll be a show all right, miss.

Havensbeck ain't been open to us since I were a little girl, but I remembers."

Bernie mused over this as she ate her breakfast with quick sharp bites. This was the first year that Haven had opened its doors to the village at Christmastime since the tragic death of its lady and heir. Could it be that Lord Matthias was emerging at last from his deep mourning?

Simon seemed to be pondering the same question. "Do you think it was Jasper who got him to open the manor?"

Bernie slid a glance toward her all too observant little brother. "I think it's none of our business." Then she relented a bit. "But he clearly loves his people. He likely just wants to give them a nice treat for Christmas."

Simon narrowed his eyes at his plate as he chewed a giant mouthful of salted ham. When he swallowed, he looked at Bernie with wry assessment. "I bet someone told him he should have a new wife. I bet someone said, your lordship, sir, it's about time you found yourself a new wife and you should probably have a big ball and see what kind of nice girls are out there in the world. And then you should pick one who is kind of pretty and kind of smart and has dresses that are tight in the bosom."

Bernie didn't laugh. Much. Still, she managed to shake her finger and give her brother a quelling glare.

"Do *not* let Aunt Sarah hear you speak so!"

Simon rolled his eyes, but his cheeks did grow pink. He glanced around them to make sure he had not been overheard. Then he grinned at his sister. "I only say things like that to you. You know that."

"I know, beastie. But the Lord of Havensbeck is truly not our concern. We are here because Aunt Sarah and Uncle Isaiah wanted to visit with John Barton."

Simon smirked at that. "You really don't think that's why, do you?"

"No, I don't." Bernie fought back a sigh, and pushed her fork through the remains of her eggs. Her appetite had abruptly faded. She didn't know what she was going to do about the John Barton situation. It didn't help that he was all things astonishing. He was smart, kind, rather unbelievably handsome, had a good position, and clearly cared deeply about Vicar Goodrich and his family.

Sudden restlessness stirred her from her comfortable chair before the fire and she pushed her plate away. "Come along, lazybones! Were you not the one bouncing on my bed half an hour past, eager to go out of doors?"

Simon shoveled three more bites of egg into his mouth even as his body went into motion. With a last grand swipe of his napkin he wiped his mouth and flung the cloth ceremoniously down onto the table. "Ready!"

AFTER THE WARMTH of the inn and the filling breakfast, so much richer than their normal winter fare, Bernie and Simon scarcely felt the cold. The morning was bright and crystalline with new-fallen snow. Full bellies and youth went a long way to cheering one up, Bernie decided.

Simon wanted to see the river. They walked down the lane out of the village and clumped through the fresh snow to the river. Simon leaned far over the bank with his arms dangling, while Bernie kept a grip on the back of his bulky jacket.

"It doesn't look like our river," he said, straightening up with doubt wrinkling his nose.

Bernie gave his shoulder a shove with her mitten-covered fist.

"It isn't our river, not yet. It's narrow and faster. And likely colder, flowing down from the high escarpment, the Roaches, the way it does. We don't get such ice in our valley."

Simon was satisfied with that explanation, but it only prompted more questions. "I want to get closer. The ice is so thick on each side. Will it freeze all the way over? Will it keep running underneath? Are there still fish in it? Why aren't they frozen?"

Bernie answered as sensibly as she could, for she was busy picking her way down the long path along the bank. It had been in use for so long it was nearly a lane, but the fresh snow didn't mingle well with long skirts. Bernie wistfully eyed Simon's canvas breeches, tucked into oilcloth gaiters halfway down his shins that went down into his sturdy walking boots.

Her own practical short boots weren't much different, but not even a dozen layers of muslin and wool could keep the wind from shivering its way up a woman's skirt.

She was so busy complaining in her mind that she walked right into Simon, who stood still in the center of the path, looking ahead and up.

Bernie followed his gaze. When she saw the dark form standing on the carriage bridge upriver, she made a grab for Simon's shoulder and dragged him back behind a slender elm.

"It's him! Bernie, it is him!"

"Yes," she answered from between gritted teeth. "I can see that."

Simon twisted out of her grasp and sidled halfway round the tree trunk, so he could see the bridge.

"He's up so early! I thought lords slept all day. I would, if I was a lord!"

Bernie wondered if she ought to tell Simon that some adults didn't actually go to bed until nearly dawn, but that would lead to questions about carousing and such and she wasn't well informed enough herself to really answer those satisfactorily, not that she would, of course. Still, a vicar's household, while it saw a great deal of other people's suffering, did tend to lead a restricted life of its own.

"Don't let him see you!"

Simon was gone. Bernie looked around wildly, only to see that he'd ducked along the path to the next elm. She could see his little multi-colored cap just on the other side of the nearby tree.

He looked back over his shoulder at her, his eyes wide. "He has a bottle!"

At that, Bernie flattened herself against her own tree and peered around the trunk. A letter? Blast it. She wouldn't be able to look for the bottle until they returned to Green Dell, and what if it smashed up against the dam until it broke, just waiting for her to come home and fetch it out?

The bottle sailed toward them to land with a splash in the river between them and the bridge.

And there it went, bobbing away in the swift current, knocking this way and that along the edges of the thick ice forming a distinct frozen edge to the bank.

The flash of varicolored knitting caught her eye, heading downriver.

"Oh!" She hissed. "I am going to put you in dresses and braid your hair for this, Simon Arthur Goodrich!"

For it was Simon she saw, running full speed down the bank path after the retreating bottle. Bernie spared one glance up at the bridge before she hiked up her skirt and ran after her rotten little maniac of a brother.

He was only chasing the bottle to see where it went, surely. He was a smart lad, too smart to do anything so foolish as to go onto the ice. But he did.

Blast, blast and triple blast! The little idiot was belly down, moving out on the ice, crawling toward the thinning edge where the bobbing bottle was cast in an eddy.

"Simon! Simon! Get back!" She ran, calling and hoping that the ice would bear her own weight long enough for her to crawl out after him, drag him back by one ankle and possibly kill him herself.

She never had the chance to find out. Just as she fell to her knees on the first few feet of the ice near the bank, she felt it. There was nothing to hear but the hiss and rush of the water driven to new speed by the narrowing banks, until the great, resonating crack of the ice rang through her entire body as if she'd pressed herself to a brass gong.

Chapter 8

I N HORROR, SHE watched helplessly as Simon, trapped on a chunk of ice the length of his body, began to move away from the bank. The dark water churned and rushed between them, the gap growing wider by the second.

"*SIMON!*" Bernie had never been one to scream, but she screamed then. Even as she scrambled and slithered toward her endangered brother, she shrieked his name with such force that she felt the raw pain of it in her throat.

It didn't matter. Her knees, nearly bare on the ice, didn't matter. Her hands, protected only by her mittens, didn't matter. She crawled and slid and flattened herself like a worm, struggling to move closer and closer. "*Simon, hold on!*"

He hadn't gone far. His ice raft had turned as it entered the current and now was lodged across the rushing Churnet like a stopper in a bottle. She could see Simon clinging to the top of the ice using his hands and feet like calipers to hold him to the ice. But the water was so cold! His fingers would freeze and he would lose his grip for certain unless she could just reach!

A DARK FORM sailed over her, a great bear of a man in a dark coat scrabbled along the ice like a four-legged demon, very nearly skating in his urgency.

Bernie saw him reach for Simon with one brawny arm, his hand outstretched like the talons of an eagle.

That large hand snatched her little bother off his little ice floe and flung him backward.

Simon spun spread-eagle across the ice like a wheel, slithering away from the river, until he came to rest on the brush-studded edge of the snowy shore. Bernie scrambled to him, careless of her own danger from the crumbling ice.

When she reached him, she grabbed each of his mitten-covered hands and shoved them inside her coat to warm against her belly. He would lose his fingers if she couldn't warm them in time.

It was only then that she thought to look over her shoulder for the man.

Her eyes found him at last. He was dragging himself back onto the ice. As she watched, the lip of ice beneath his belly crumbled away and he began to slip into the rushing water.

She couldn't leave Simon. But she couldn't let her brother's savior drown or freeze, or both!

She pulled off her coat and rolled her brother up quickly into it like a sausage, so that no part of him was exposed.

Leaving him behind, his muffled protests nearly inaudible, she slithered back out onto the ice as far as she dared. It would do no one any good for her to fall into the river now!

She grabbed her long scarf and unwound it from her neck. "Here!" she shouted over the rushing water. "Grab this!"

Luckily, the scarf, made from bits and scraps of yarn saved up over the course of a year, was tightly knitted and very long. And luckier still, the man had more presence of mind that had a frightened eight-year-old boy.

He caught the end of the scarf on the first try and wrapped it around his wrist by twisting his hand. Bernie had no hope of towing him free, but she could at least try to give him something to pull against.

She held the band of knitted wool in both fists and braced her feet in front of her, leaning back against the pull of his weight that threatened to drag her out onto the dangerously thin ice.

When her boot heels caught on a ridge of ice, she used her whole body, tensing like a bow with the scarf as her bowstring. The man used the leverage given by his handhold on the scarf to worm his way onto the ice on his elbows, then his belly, then his knees. At last, he crawled to the edge of the earthen bank and staggered to his feet.

When the tension eased on the scarf, Bernie rolled away, abandoning him in a great hurry to get back to Simon now that their savior had been himself saved.

After she'd assured herself that Simon was indeed warming up, she bound him even more tightly into her coat and stood, lifting him into her arms like a sack of flour.

Her throat closed tight in gratitude. He was getting heavier every month. And now, thanks to the man before her, Simon would continue to do so, would grow and learn and survive, at least until she got him back to the inn. There, she fully intended to murder him herself!

Bernie turned to the man of mystery, only to look up into the furious gaze of Lord Matthias Waterford of Havensbeck Manor. Oh.

"What the bloody hell do you mean by letting the child play on the ice!"

His dark sapphire eyes were brilliant. His fury only made them brighter. Bernie studied this as if she were watching him from far away. He loomed over her and his tension was obvious. She should have been alarmed or at least inclined to step back from him. Her relief at Simon's rescue and her deep gratitude to this man made her unafraid.

Instead she put out one hand to him while hefting Simon higher on her shoulder with the other.

"I love my brother. I would do anything for him. But no one can watch a child every single moment."

He flinched from her as violently as if she had burned him with her touch. "You say that because you are not a parent!"

"No, I am not. Merely a deeply committed sister." She smiled at him. "I can see you're truly upset with me. However, right now I would pretty much do anything for you, as well."

He stared at her. "What a strange thing to say to me."

MATTHIAS DIDN'T THINK she was offering what it sounded like she was offering. From her level gaze, he surmised that she was much too innocent to understand how odd she sounded. She was a virtuous woman, from a respectable household. The shadows in her eyes came from pain and loss, but not from jaded knowledge.

Marianna had been like that. She'd said the most outrageous things, yet her obvious innocence and inner joy had turned her blunt outspokenness into charming vulnerability.

His emotions roiled within him. Fear for the boy had stirred old ghosts into raging demons of loss. One child lost. One child saved.

The world hinged on such tiny moments, on the crack of ice, or the tip of a candle.

It was all too much. He wanted to flee this woman, her clear gaze and her little Simon. He wanted to wrap her in his arms and keep her forever. He wanted to go back to being a young man with joy in his heart. Or perhaps he wanted to be old, with his loss dimmed and dulled by the years between.

He didn't know what he was thinking. He was an idiot, standing here staring at a coatless young woman holding a soaked shivering child while he dripped icy water from his sodden clothing. "Come to the house."

He plucked the exhausted Simon from her grasp and tucked him against his own chest. Without another word he turned to start back up the river path to where he joined the carriage lane by the bridge. She could follow him or not, but he knew she would.

Bernie scrambled quickly after him. Of course, he was right. They had to get Simon warm and dry at once. She was suddenly very aware of her damp and dirty gown. By the time they reached the manor she began to shiver. The door opened as they approached and the footman rushed out to take Simon from his lordship. Even as Bernie entered the grand foyer of the manor, a chambermaid bustled forward with a blanket and swept it over her shoulders. A small man with sharp features rounded everyone up briskly.

"Higgins, take the young lady to the blue room! I'll have a tub brought up at once for the boy."

The maid firmly removed Bernie from the hall and before she knew it she was halfway up the stairs. She halted and half-turned. "But Simon --"

The fellow, who could only be Jasper the butler, didn't smile at her but his expression was reassuring. "The young man will be in the room next to yours, Miss Goodrich," he assured her. "Now go."

Such was his manner of command that she began to climb the stairs again without actually thinking about it. The maid led her into a beautiful room and after laying the fire in the fireplace of creamy stone, began to strip her wet things from her. Yet all Bernie could think was one thing.

She knew all about Jasper. Yet how had Jasper known her name?

EVEN AS WEARY as he was, Simon rebelled at the notion of being bathed by the pert Havensbeck chambermaid. Bernie rolled her eyes, rolled up her borrowed dressing gown sleeves and, after dismissing the young woman, tossed her rotten, precious little brother into the steaming water. He yelped.

"Time for another dunking, me lad, and no complaints from you!" She scowled as she poured a pitcher of water over his head.

He came up sputtering. "Bernie, I had to get the bottle!"

"Well, you nearly died trying!" She worked a handful of rather fine soap into his hair as she scolded him. "If his lordship hadn't been there—"

Simon pushed her hands away and gave his own head a scrubbing. "I'm not a baby!" Before she could pour another pitcher of water, he dunked himself in the tub to rinse.

When she came at him with a wash cloth, he held up both hands to stop her. "I'm clean! It was ice, Bernie, not mud!"

He was so little, sitting there in the giant copper tub, looking up at her with dark shadows of exhaustion beneath his eyes. Bernie's fury left her. In its wake there remained only her terror.

He might have died. I couldn't save him. Were it not for Lord Matthias, I would have lost him.

She buried her face in the cloth and fought the sobs that threatened to rip through her.

"Aw, Bernie!"

Without lifting her head, she stuck out one arm and pointed at the bed.

It was a mark of how weary he was that he did not protest a nap. She kept her face in her hands and listened to him slosh his way out of the tub, dry off and pad over to the vast bed.

"I haven't a nightshirt—"

She could only make a strangled gulping noise but he seemed to understand that now was not the time to debate the notion of sleeping in his skin.

At last, when the room was quiet but for Simon's deep breathing and the snap of the coals in the hearth, Bernie allowed the tears. When she'd wept every remnant of her fear and panic away, she was left calm and empty. She dried her face on the cloth and straightened.

Simon's bath had gone lukewarm. She could ring for a fresh one for herself, but the thought of all the servants trouping in and out made her go a bit weak in the knees. Fortunately, the maid had left two more pitchers of water warming by the fire. Bernie rolled the cloth around her hand to protect it from the hot pewter handles and carried them one at a time to pour into the bath.

Then she stripped quickly, hung her dressing gown over a chair by the fire and slipped into the bath. Not hot, but pleasantly warm. The water soaked the last of her chill away and the elegant floral-scented soap dispensed with the last remnant of river smell.

How divine. She didn't get many hot baths in the middle of winter, and never in a tub she could lie down in. She lay back against the warm copper back and gazed upward.

The ceiling was decorated with a frieze of blue sky and clouds, surrounded by a carved trim gleaming with gilt. It was nonsense, of course. Bernie could hear Aunt Sarah now. *A pointless luxury to be enjoyed by the useless. A sin when there is so much work to be done!*

It was also joyous, and pleasing, and harmless, as far as Bernie could see. What was wrong with pretty things? If one *must* have a thing, like a ceiling for instance, was it not a celebration of heaven's gifts to make it a beautiful thing?

One could go too far, of course, and value things too highly, or deprive others for the sake of mere objects, but Bernie did not get the impression that Lord Matthias thought overmuch of his possessions.

What did he think of, other than the past?

Was he a good master? The village was prosperous and the estate well-kept. Was that a sign of a thoughtful man, or merely an efficient one?

The water cooled too soon and Bernie had to rise reluctantly from her treat to dry before her chill returned. Her gown and underthings were nearly dry, but for the hem and cuffs, so she donned them once more. For a moment, she gazed longingly at the wide bed and the rather small boy using only a portion of it. Then she shook off her languor.

She wasn't a guest here. She was flotsam, washed up by the river. It wouldn't do to take advantage.

So instead of a nap, she set herself to leaving the room as she had found it. Mostly, that task consisted of mopping up water from the floor and tidying the towels and soap.

On the table by the bed, the maid who had taken away Simon's soaked clothing had left a small pile of Simon's belongings. It was the usual collection one might find in a boy's pockets; a wobbly marble, a brass rivet from a harness, a small river stone with a hole worn in it, a handkerchief that greatly needed washing, a wad of sodden paper.

Bernie picked up the handkerchief with two fingers and took it to swish out in the bathwater. Then she hung it on the fire guard to dry.

The paper gave her pause, however. There was something familiar about the size and shape of the rolled wad.

As she peeled away the layers to reveal the blurred lines of all too familiar script, Bernie's heart began to pound.

Simon had gone after the bottle. Somehow in the middle of the danger and commotion, he'd managed to uncork the glass and pull the letter free. Her little brother had a cool head on him, that was certain.

That determination had nearly cost him his life. If she were a proper adult, with an appropriate notion of child-rearing, she would toss the entire mess into the fire and let it steam until it caught.

Instead, she spent several long minutes peeling back sheet by sheet, laying them on the warm stones of the hearth.

I want to know.

IT IS A bright winter this year. The sun rides low but lovely in a clear sky. The snowfall is dry and crystalline, so unlike the heavy wet snows of that year that slowed my way home.

It seems so cruel that something as small as a snowflake had the power to take you from me. A tiny snowflake, heavy instead of light, multiplied by the millions to block the road, to weigh down my carriage, to drive a chill gloom so deep into our home that only the rash use of candles could hold back the darkness.

And when the fire blazed, where was all that wet and damp to suppress its ravenous flame? Hateful winter, to take such vengeance upon us.

A dark season. A bright season. I know not how to embrace this glittering lovely world without you in it. All my abandoned winters have seemed so dark before. I do not fit rightly within this brilliant time.

I need answers, my darling. There must be answers to all the world's questions where you are. Pray, spare some for a dark man unsure of the light.

Chapter 9

N O ONE CAME for the bath. Bernie waited quietly, with Simon snoring lightly in the big bed and the nearly dry letter in her lap.

She had no fear of being caught with it. After all, it was only a few sheets of paper that could be anything at all. Moreover, she'd practiced folding it lengthwise and sliding it into her sleeve so many times that she was quite confident she could do so at the merest turn of the latch.

I am becoming sadly deceptive.

Part of her was ashamed. That was the part that took all Aunt Sarah's admonitions to heart. The part that believed in fair play, honesty and high virtue.

The other part, the one that kept all of Lord Matthias's letters in the bottom of her sewing case, the one that read and re-read them long after Simon had fallen asleep, the part that had wanted to come to Haven even after learning of the author's high rank and tragic loss.

She didn't mean to be conniving. There was simply some part of her that clung to the outlandish notion that those letters had been meant for her to find, that upriver was a man who needed a friend, and that possibly, just possibly, that friend might be her.

This was the fantasy that had kept her warm during the harsh winters at the vicarage, had made it easier to smile at her brother when loss and responsibility threatened to weigh her down, had given her something to look forward to year after year when her unchanging life seemed likely to remain yet the same forevermore.

I need answers, my darling.

A bolt of restlessness shot through her at the thought. She stood to pace before the hearth, folding and unfolding the pages in her hands.

She needed to get out of this room.

Simon would be fine. It was a grand house, full of earnestly helpful staff. If anything, the manor should fear Simon and his ambition to see and know everything there was to know about everything.

For a second, she savored this relative lack of responsibility. Simon was safe. He was clean and dry and asleep. There was even a tray of buttered bread and pickles laid out for him when he awoke.

Mentally dusting her hands, Bernie opened the door as silently as possible and set out to explore the manor.

ONE END OF the long hallway led to another hall which led to the grand staircase. Since Bernie had no desire to see the front hall again, she went in the other direction.

This led to a grand gallery. One side of the long wide room seemed made of light. The windows were wide and high, larger than even the glass in the Green Dell chapel.

At first she found her gaze drawn by the magnificent views of the estate grounds. She faced the drive, a long gravel lane that looped on itself in front of the great doorway, so visiting carriages could turn easily.

Stretching out before the house were long beds of flowers—or at least, they would bloom come spring. Now they were like the straight bones of some giant creature slumbering just under the snow. Only the dormant branches of the maze stretched high enough to pierce the fallen snow, reaching up like a gray-brown memory of the green walls of summer.

It was austere and chilling to see, yet Bernie could imagine the life just below the surface, ready to burst forth once the season turned, pulling off the still white blanket of winter.

"I fear it looks a bit grim now," said a voice over Bernie's shoulder.

She jumped a little, then turned to see the smiling face of the Havensbeck butler.

"Jasper—I mean, Mr. Jasper—"

"Jasper is fine, Miss Goodrich."

It wasn't fine, not really. But she was in the awkward position of not-quite-guest so she took the nice man at his word.

"Thank you, Jasper." She waved a hand at the window. "I was just thinking about," she was going to sound odd but the words just kept coming, "blankets."

But Jasper's eyes crinkled slightly. "Yes, miss. I quite see what you mean. Everything is caught in a spell of slumber, so to speak."

She let out a breathy laugh. "Precisely!"

"Is young Master Simon resting well?"

Bernie nodded. "He's a terror to put to bed, but once there he falls like a sawn tree. There'll be no waking him until he's ready."

Oh dear. She sounded as if she were fishing for an invitation to stay the night. "But I'm sure it won't be long until he's up and about," she assured the kindly butler. "And we'll be on our way." *And out of yours.*

"I hope the staff took good care of your needs," he said as he turned her from the end of the hall back toward the gallery. She wasn't quite sure how he managed it, for he didn't so much as touch her elbow, but suddenly they were perusing the paintings instead of the view.

"The lords of Havensbeck make up quite a roguish band," Jasper said. Bernie had the impression he was continuing a conversation they'd never actually held. Odd, but reassuring. She wasn't the only pudding-head about the place.

She gazed obediently at the first painting. It was a life-size portrait of a man in a suit of armor. She squinted at it. "Didn't they weave tapestries back then, not paint canvas?"

"Oh, this isn't a portrait of a medieval knight. It's only Lord Burgess stuffed into some ancestral loot. His current lordship's great-great-uncle, that is. He hated the fashion of the day, with those puffy pumpkin breeches—"

"Paned slops," Bernie corrected him absently.

"Indeed. So he had the artist paint him in the armor instead. Claimed he wouldn't be preserved for posterity with a—pardon me, miss, but it is a quote—'fat arse'."

Bernie smiled. "And is that why he is a 'rogue'?"

"Oh no, Miss Goodrich. He was a rogue because he was a cattle thief, of sorts. Whenever he visited another household, he would bring his 'pet' cow. No one could protest such a little thing, no matter how odd it seemed. It wasn't until years later that he confessed that it was a different cow every time and that he was simply avoiding breeding fees, while tucking into his victim's banquets and paying court to their daughters."

Bernie bit her lip against a laugh. Jasper was being rather salty but she supposed that came of having no lady about the house.

She moved on to the next portrait, a brooding fellow with a long dark wig and a thin mustache. His bulky black velvet coat was absolutely festooned with tatting. "And this one? Was he a secret highwayman or a rum smuggler?"

"Not rum. Lace," Jasper responded promptly.

Bernie frowned. "He smuggled lace?"

"Oh yes. You see, at that time King Charles II was in the midst of a little tiff with the Flemish. To build England's lace trade the monarchy placed an embargo on Brussels lace. Lord Kern didn't wish to be without his frippery, so he shipped over a bit for himself and his friends. It became so lucrative that he rebuilt the family coffers twice over before the embargo was finally lifted."

"And no one ever knew?"

"Of course they knew! How else would they get their lace? The king himself was a customer."

Bernie shook her head. "Politics."

Jasper nodded sagely. "Politics."

Bernie's gaze lingered on Lord Kern's sleeves as they moved on. Aunt Sarah didn't believe in bold ornamentation. Mama had liked it very well.

I miss lace.

"Berrrrniiiiie!" Simon's howl echoed through the upper halls of the great house.

Jasper's eyes widened. "Oh my. He must be hurt!" He turned to hurry toward the bedchamber.

Bernie let out a sigh as she followed him, brisk but not panicked. "No. That 'Bernie' sounds entirely different. This one leads me to think that some chambermaid has caught him in his altogether."

Clearly, this strange, intriguing glimpse into the life at Havensbeck Manor was over. It was time to get herself and her wee beastie back where they belonged. Bernie only hoped she and Simon could keep Aunt and Uncle from taking their adventures too much to heart and calling an end to their holiday altogether.

In this, she knew Simon would be a solid co-conspirator.

THE NEXT MORNING, even Aunt Sarah had been distracted from her previous evening's disapproval by the Christmas Eve Ball at Havensbeck Manor. She wasn't the only one. By the time Bernie had progressed from her room at the inn, down the stairs and into the dining room, no less than a dozen people had asked if they would see her there.

The chambermaid for her room told her all about the gown she planned to wear as she filled the coal scuttle by the hearth. An elderly guest in the upstairs hall begged a dance with a teasing twinkle in his eye. A trio of giggling young women on the stairs informed Bernie, although she'd not asked, that they would be happy to help her with her hair.

"Not that there's any little thing actually *wrong* with it, of course!"

"Oh, no! It's just that we have *ideas!*"

Bernie decided the correct response to all of the above was, "That sounds lovely."

At their table, where Uncle Isaiah, Aunt Sarah, and Simon had already taken their seats, Bernie found an large, embossed invitation placed at a graceful angle across her plate. Simon was a-wiggle with curiosity and even Aunt Sarah couldn't take her gaze from the heavy parchment square as she nibbled on her toast.

Bernie sat at her place and plucked her napkin from its folds to lay it painstakingly across her lap, as if she had no idea what they were waiting for. Then she smiled calmly at her family. "Good morning, everyone! My, the baking smells delicious today."

Uncle Isaiah twinkled at her playful torture, but Aunt Sarah huffed. "Oh, you impossible child!"

Bernie thought Simon would snicker at her little game, but his gaze was still riveted on the invitation. "Openit-openit-openit," he whispered under his breath.

Of course Bernie was more eager than anyone to find out what it was, but her nature could be a bit on the contrary side. It seemed she never wanted to do something if someone else deeply wanted her to do it.

Besides, she knew who had sent the invitation. At least, she thought she knew. And if it was who she thought it was, it wasn't the one she wished it was.

I'm not contrary. I'm insane.

Her natural common sense reasserted itself with a snap. Without further play, she picked up the heavy folded sheet and carefully lifted the plain amber-colored wax seal from the paper without breaking it.

"Dear Miss Goodrich,

I hope this finds you in good health. I regret that I could not converse properly with you yesterday. It is my hope that you intend to grace with your presence the Christmas Eve Ball at Havensbeck tonight. Although your attendance will be reward enough, it is my dearest wish that you might charitably grant to me a waltz."

Bernie closed the invitation and slipped it discreetly to her lap beneath the table. Then she looked up at her companions.

Simon looked confused. Uncle Isaiah wore his raised brows like an unfamiliar hat. Aunt Sarah, on the other hand, gazed at Bernie with very wide eyes.

"My goodness," she breathed. Then she blinked and shook off her amazement, trying to look blasé. "I had no idea young John Barton was so articulate."

Eloquent. Gracious.

Romantic.

Bernie forced a light smile. "Neither had I."

Beneath the table, she slid her fingers across the raised design of the seal. It was a simple mark, a shape really. Nothing but a trio of curved lines, as might denote something on a map. A road, perhaps. If one hadn't see the graceful calligraphy closure at the bottom of the letter, one might have no idea what it signified. A river.

In hope, your grateful host.

M.

MATTHIAS RIPPED HIS cravat loose yet again. "Blasted thing!" He'd meant to roar the words. Instead, he sounded frantic to his own ears.

Jasper, who had just entered the master's bedchamber with a tray of coffee in his gloved hands and three freshly ironed cravats over his arm, gave Matthias a glance of veiled exasperation. At least, Matthias imagined that he did. He was certainly exasperated with himself.

He dropped his head and held out the snarled cravat in defeat. "I cannot do it. Rescue me."

"Certainly, my lord."

Jasper stepped before him and turned him away from the mirror. Matthias peered downward over his own nose, trying to see what his butler was doing.

"Stop trying to look, my lord. You're denting the folds."

"Oh, well. Haven forbid I dent the folds." But Matthias gazed at the ceiling obediently anyway.

It only took Jasper seconds to do what Matthias had been failing at for a quarter of an hour. Normally, Matthias had no trouble dressing himself, tying his day-to-day linen cravats with the simplest of knots. This independence had led his creatively-starved valet to seek other employment years ago.

The formal silk cravat was another story, it seemed. Matthias examined Jasper's handiwork in the mirror. "This looks intricate." It was snug and high and uncomfortable, that was for certain. Matthias felt as though he should continue to gaze at the ceiling if he wanted to breathe properly.

"It is the current mode, my lord. Right to the minute."

"Ah." Matthias backed down before Jasper's fashion sense. "As long as it isn't yesterday's style. You know I cannot bear to be twenty-four hours behind the latest fashion."

Jasper ignored Matthias's mockery. "Me neither, my lord."

He poured Matthias a cup of blisteringly hot coffee. Black and harsh, the way he'd learned to drink it in the West Indies.

That tropical place was a memory so distant that it seemed a fairytale in this wintry Sussex valley. Matthias gazed absently at the tracings of frost that clouded the glass of his bedchamber window, turning the view of white, mounded landscape into a crystalline outline.

"She laughs," he told Jasper without turning. "But she is an orphan. How does she laugh when she's lost so much?"

Jasper looked up from placing the fresh cravats in their proper drawer.

"Perchance it requires practice, my lord." Jasper never gave in to maudlin emotion, but Matthias heard the faint trace of compassion in his butler's cool tone.

"Yes, perchance it does." He couldn't imagine ever feeling light enough to laugh. Laughter required some buoyancy of spirit, and Matthias's very feet felt as though they were made of lead. Most days it was all he could do to keep them moving forward.

Jasper turned as he left the bedchamber. "Like many things, my lord, perhaps the first time is the hardest."

Chapter 10

B ERNIE SAT NEXT to Aunt Sarah in the sturdy carriage that Haven had provided for John Barton's use. John and Uncle Isaiah sat across from her, as gentlemen did, taking the rear-facing, less comfortable seats.

John caught Bernie's gaze and issued her a self-conscious smile. She nodded politely back with an awkward smile of her own. Next to her, Aunt Sarah rustled with repressed urgency. Never had Bernie felt under such scrutiny! How could she ever learn if she liked someone if every single twitch was noted in some sort of matchmaker scorebook?

Dancing later would be better. Bernie tucked her arms inside her cape and folded them beneath her bosom. Her bodice felt too tight. This had been her last silk gown from her life before. She and Aunt Sarah had ripped it out and remade it into this one two years earlier.

The pale green silk still fit fairly well, although her eighteen-year-old bosom had been a little smaller. Bernie felt restricted, as if Aunt Sarah had sewn her chaperoning vigilance into every seam.

Which was an unfair thought. Aunt Sarah had done her best, spending evening after evening painstakingly snipping threads in order to salvage the greatest portion of fine fabric. Then she and Bernie had spent hours poring over pattern books, trying to find just the right cut that would complement Bernie's new height and figure, and put the reclaimed silk to best use.

The result was this simple gown. The once fuller skirts had been remade into a slender column, allowing the extra fabric to be used to lengthen it. The old ruched bodice had been ironed out and used for the cap sleeves, and the new bodice, made from diagonally pieced squares, was plain but for a running thread of darker green embroidery, simple leaves and vines climbing the lattice pattern. Bernie had never had time to progress past her early ladylike accomplishments into flowers and intricate animal figures, like the ones her mother had done with such skill.

"No matter," Aunt Sarah had told her briskly at the time. "The gown is still finer than any I've ever owned, and I've managed to keep breathing in and out."

The girlish ribbons that had once made silk bows around the hem had been picked apart and seamed into a single band, which Bernie now wore wound in her hair. She was grateful for it, for her hair tended toward rebellion at the best of times. At the moment, it was so full of pins that she felt like a hedgehog.

Of course, she was well aware that she was focusing on these tiny discomforts to conceal the great galloping nervous excitement that threatened to make her leap from her seat and pick up her skirts to race ahead of the sedate team pulling the carriage.

Wouldn't Aunt Sarah twitch then?

Her First Ball. That was the only reason for her excitement, of course. She had spent the afternoon forcing Simon to dance with her, turning about their inn room, bumping into chairs, trying to remember everything she could from Mama's playful lessons. Papa had promised to retain a proper dancing master once she turned sixteen. Of course, that had not happened.

Still, she knew all the country dances. Assemblies might be few and far between in hardworking Green Dell, but even poor farmers liked to kick up their heels occasionally.

But the quadrille and the waltz were distant memories and Bernie feared she would not recall the steps when in the reputedly grand ballroom of Havensbeck.

And in his arms.

No. Stop thinking that. His note was simply friendly. She was new in town and the lord of the manor was merely being gentlemanly. She'd heard gossip from the chambermaids at the inn that Lord Matthias likely wouldn't even attend. And if he did, no one believed he would stay long. Certainly no one thought he would dance.

Except he asked me to dance. He wrote it down, right there in the invitation.

Her belly flipped at the memory of those words.

The handwriting had been more decorous and fine than that contained in the long anguished letters from the river, but it had been the same, she told herself. Simon thought so, although "less drunken" was perhaps not a sufficient reason for the difference.

She wished she could take it out and look at it again, as she had a hundred times today. However, she dared not bring her aunt to comment upon it to John Barton, who apparently had no awareness that the older couple believed him to be her correspondent.

Although your attendance will be reward enough, it is my dearest wish that you might charitably grant to me a waltz.

Oh, would this carriage ride never end?

MATTHIAS SENSED THE very air grow warmer in the ballroom, as if he felt the touch of sunlight on his skin on a cloudy day. He turned, aware that the rest of the guests had also looked up suddenly, as though the guest of honor had arrived at last.

Or perhaps it was only he who awaited her. He felt as if he'd been waiting for years.

Which was ridiculous. He hadn't even known of her until a few days before. And yet there she was.

Bernadette.

She was very different from the canvas-bound girl in the plain bonnet and the mis-knitted gloves.

Now, Miss Bernadette Goodrich stood in a gown so elegant it was very nearly severe. She was indeed tall enough to lend a regal air to the fullness of her figure. Still, her unmistakable smile beamed out at them all. He felt as if she had invited them all to *her* ball and now glowed her welcome.

Her hand still remain tucked into the young vicar's elbow. Matthias felt a jolt, seeing her on another man's arm. However, Barton was a family friend. Of course she would arrive with the vicar, along with her aunt and uncle.

Perhaps he was like a brother to her.

Keep telling yourself that.

Matthias thought the fellow looked mightily proud of himself, walking into the ball with such a prize on his arm.

You felt like that once, remember?

The dark thought rose and then washed pale and silent, the shadow fading in the light of Bernadette's smile upon him. Matthias stepped forward, catching her eye and bowing deeply. As he'd hoped, she released Barton's arm to issue a low curtsy of her own in return. When she straightened, she clasped her hands before her as she waited for his approach, now standing slightly apart from the vicar.

Matthias thought he'd done that rather neatly, and hoped that no one had noticed. "Miss Goodrich. You came. You're here."

She laughed a little. "Yes, Lord Matthias. And you are here as well, at your own ball."

She laughed at him. Well, it was true he was acting the loon. He didn't care one little bit.

John Barton cleared his throat. Matthias tore his gaze away from Bernadette. Her eyes snapped green fire in the candlelight, how captivating! He forced a civil nod to the vicar, who was, after all, his very own vicar, a good man carefully chosen for Haven's greatest benefit.

"Hello, Barton." His welcome sounded rather lackluster. *Must do something about that.* "You're here, as well."

Barton was looking at him, or rather, through him, as if inspecting a seed in his glass of lemonade. Whatever the vicar saw made him lift his hand as if to snatch Bernadette back into his custody. He caught himself and folded his hands behind his back, clearly dismayed at his reaction.

So the vicar *was* courting her.

Bernadette, however, stood equidistant between the two men, her bright gaze taking in the bedecked ballroom, oblivious to raised hackles or any other sort of territorial conduct. If Miss Goodrich was being courted, she showed no awareness of it.

She has no idea he fancies her.

Matthias didn't allow his thoughts to progress any further down the notion of who else might fancy the cheerful Miss Bernadette Goodrich.

"The staff has outdone themselves on the decorations," he said, although he'd barely glanced at them. Then he had an inspired notion. "And the tables are absolutely laden with refreshments and cakes."

The emerald gaze fixed on him instantly. "Cakes?"

Matthias nodded and turned a bland gaze upon Barton. *I am lord of this hall. I do not fetch cake.* The vicar shot him a grim, defeated glance, then bowed smartly to Miss Goodrich. "Would you care for something, Bernie?"

Perhaps Barton sought to underscore his familiarity with the use of that family nickname, but Matthias, painfully alert to her every expression, saw Bernadette draw back slightly at the diminutive.

Matthias understood something in that instant. "Bernie" was the girl who wore thick shapeless coats and scampered in the snow with her little brother. Tonight Miss Goodrich wanted to be something more. Not someone else, precisely, but beyond simple Bernie. As she had every right to. Tonight, she was without a doubt a grown woman, regal and refined. A woman named *Bernadette.*

When she replied to the vicar, her tone cooled ever so slightly. "If you please, John. Cake and, hmm."

"Champagne?" Matthias suggested.

"Truly?" Bernadette's eyes widened as she glanced about for her aunt. Matthias enjoyed her moment of lip-chewing indecision. "Well perhaps, hmm, later, if there is to be a toast."

Barton nodded pedantically. "Much more appropriate for a young lady."

When Miss Goodrich and Matthias turned on him with equally narrowed gazes, Barton stepped back, bobbed a quick bow that encompassed them both, and strode away.

Matthias thought he heard Miss Goodrich mutter, "It had best be a *large* piece of cake."

Lord Matthias leaned down closer. "Your aunt and uncle, I presume?"

Bernie turned to follow his gesture to where an older couple stood with the innkeeper and his wife. "Yes, that is Uncle Isaiah and Aunt Sarah."

They looked just a bit thunderstruck by the elegance of their surroundings.

"Your cake, Bernie."

Matthias turned to see John Barton at his elbow. Back so soon? How conscientious. The young vicar handed a plate with a sliver of pastry upon it to Miss Goodrich. He cast Matthias a slightly victorious look.

"My lord, might I beg a moment of your time? We have a surprise for you!"

At that same moment, Mrs. Goodrich appeared at Bernadette's

elbow. "Bernie dear, I've found some people I would like you to meet. Such a lovely village, so very friendly!"

Matthias could only stand there as Bernadette was led away. She glanced over her shoulder at him, gave a rueful shrug, and obediently trotted after her aunt.

Matthias turned back to John. "I suspect collusion."

John Barton beamed at him innocently. "I'm sorry, my lord, but I don't understand."

"No? Well then, let us go view this surprise."

John Barton led the way to the base of the staircase to the mezzanine. Ranged upon the first half-dozen steps were a varied group of children. They looked quite ordinary to Matthias, although one assumed their parents felt differently. Some were plump and some plain, and at least one child had a very unfortunate ratio of ears to skull. Matthias didn't actually recognize any of them, but then he had hardly spoken to anyone in the village for years. For all their motley size and appearance, they all looked well-scrubbed and eager. Something was going to happen, for the guests standing around the staircase were beaming with pride and expectance at Matthias, clearly hoping for his attention and appreciation.

John Barton gave a quick double-clap and the children, who had been nudging and elbowing each other and generally behaving like children, immediately stopped and stood still. Matthias watched as John Barton raised both hands and begin to wave them in the air like a conjurer.

And, just like magic, sweet choral music came from the throats of the children. Their high voices rang like bells in the grand ballroom.

Matthias held very still as the children's chorus wound through an ancient carol, singing of the holly and the ivy with breathtaking purity in their piping voices. Matthias was spellbound at the sheer unlikely crystalline sound emerging from such everyday beings.

And he waited for it to hurt.

It did, a little. He thought of his own little Simon, and wondered if his son would've stood on the steps right this moment with these carol-singers at the Christmas ball. He thought of Marianna and how much she would've enjoyed this performance. He also thought of skinny little Simon Goodrich and how the children before him all looked much more well-fed and prosperous.

By the time the song ended, Matthias's thoughts had completed a harrowing circle from the past back around to the present. It was somewhat tiring, to tell the truth, this need to exist in the present. Would it ever become easier?

Nonetheless, he applauded most assiduously and as the children filed down the stairs he bent over and shook each small, perspiring hand. He did it fully aware that the entire village watched him. He also did it because the little carol-singers had clearly worked very hard on their astonishing performance and they all watched him with eyes hungry for his approval.

He was not so far gone from this world that he would ignore such a trusting gaze.

They were all very small to be so accomplished. Matthias shook his head in wonder. Clearly, John Barton was some sort of champion vicar, the sort of fellow who never settled for "good enough." A man like that must always be looking for the next obstacle, simply for the joy of overcoming it.

The children clearly obeyed Barton out of respect and affection, for they were not as subdued as they might have been had they walked in fear of their instructor. As they filed from the room a few of the boys began a cheerful shoving match, clearly energized by their success.

Matthias watched them, his sadness swimming slowly deep below his surface, like a trout beneath the ice. What sort of boy would his little Simon have been? Would he have been like the scrappy little one who gave as good as he got? Or like the older boy who was aware of the eyes upon them and quickly dragged the scrappers apart? Simon would never sing, or play, or scrap, or dash off to one side and sneak a seed cake from the refreshment table the way one little girl did on her way out.

The pain welled. The memories swirled within him. He drew himself up, suddenly tightly aware of the crowd around him.

Then his gaze found the amused and sympathetic eyes of Miss Bernadette Goodrich, where she stood on the other side of the semicircle of spectators.

Matthias felt the tension begin to drain away as he watched her smile grow. Then he noticed that Miss Goodrich stood now only with her uncle, Vicar Goodrich. John Barton and his co-conspirator Mrs.

Goodrich were nowhere in sight.

Seize the moment, yes, I will. Matthias was not about to let Miss Goodrich slip away from him again.

He dashed across the crowd so quickly that he granted himself fortunate that his boots did not skid on the marble floor when he bowed before Miss Goodrich.

"Miss Goodrich. Vicar Goodrich." He crooked one arm in her direction and indicated the dance floor with a nod of his head. "Did I not reserve a waltz for this evening?"

Miss Goodrich tilted her head. "Well, my lord, you did ask. However, I do not actually recall replying with consent."

Matthias blinked. *Um.* He had suddenly run out of words. It was certainly presumptuous to assume that a lady wished to dance simply because he'd asked. *I'm no good at this sort of thing anymore.*

Not that he ever truly had been.

Just as he was about to utter a curt apology and flee, she wrinkled her nose at him and tucked her arm into his. "So, my lord, my belated response is 'yes, thank you'."

Chapter 11

A S THEY MADE their way through the crowd to the center of the ballroom, Bernie reminded herself of her manners, but she couldn't help teasing Lord Matthias a little. He was so endearing.

It must be so for everyone who knew him. How odd now, to think she'd imagined she knew his secret self from reading all those letters. She'd been privy to his steadfast heart, his sincerity, his abiding loyalty. She had imagined those admirable traits might be hidden, somehow, sheltered behind some aloof and imposing facade.

Now she wondered if he only had a single self. An integrated, true interior that matched his exterior, the man that everyone here had seen and known for many years. How very authentic.

Oh, she *liked* this man. She wanted to do something for him, as he had done for her, giving her and everyone else this beautiful night. She had nothing to offer in return, did she? All she had in the world was herself. There was little that someone in her position could do for such a man.

She wanted to make him laugh. So far she had only succeeded in amusing herself, but that was something of a start, was it not?

With her arm on his, he continued to ease her through the crowd, who all seemed incredibly happy to see her, which was a little odd considering she'd never met most of them.

Lord Matthias's deep voice interrupted her galloping thoughts. "And where is Simon tonight?"

"Snug in his bed, under the watchful eye of Mr. Cranston's elderly mother." Bernie pursed her lips slightly. "At least, he'd better be!"

"Is he troublesome, then?"

Bernie shook her head. "Heavens, no! Just lively-minded. That's what my mother used to say. He is so curious about everything. Why does the river run down and not up? If the cows eat the grass and the people eat the cows -- " She stopped and shook her head ruefully. "Sorry, my lord. My aunt claims I can run on for days if no one remembers to shut off the sluice."

He looked down at her. "Tell me. I want to know what Simon wonders."

She bit her lip. "He asked, if the cows eat the grass and the people eat the cows, does the grass eat the people?"

Matthias surprised them both with a gruff sound that was not quite a chuckle.

Bernie hid a small gratified smile and went on. "I didn't know what to tell him. I mean to say, he is quite correct in his own way, but the thought of him ever repeating it in front of Aunt Sarah doesn't bear thinking about!"

There. She had lightened him, even if only for a moment.

And then the ballroom floor was before them. Bernie let out a sigh of admiration. Even though she knew that it was a crowd of blacksmiths and butchers, the view of the men in fine dark surcoats and their ladies in their brightest and best seemed the finest, most glittering company she could have imagined.

Lord Matthias waved his hand and the sprightly country dance tune eased to a finish. He turned to Bernie and releasing her arm, bowed deeply and offered her his hand. "Will you waltz with me, Miss Goodrich?"

Breathlessly, she put her gloved hand in his large one. When he wrapped her fingers in his, she bit her lip against the jolt of heat that jumped from the contact. Touching him was so much more than nice, or fine, or pleasant, more than merely the warmth of his hand. She felt a strange sort of familiarity twanging within her, like a bowstring released. That sense of recognition mingled with perfectly understandable attraction. Not to mention whatever it was that he bathed with that made him smell *so* good! The combination dizzied her very blood as it rushed through her.

Then the musicians began a waltz tune. Bernie's chest felt tight, so profound was her exhilaration. Lord Matthias lifted her hand in his and guided her onto the floor.

IN THE BALLROOM, Jasper circled the crowd with his silver tray until he spotted his quarry. He dove through the mob of villagers and popped up next to the elder vicar's wife.

He bowed deeply. "A fortifying drink for a chilly night, ma'am?" he offered.

Mrs. Sarah Goodrich sniffed at him. "I do not partake of spirits."

Jasper drew himself up. "And I should never offer such to a lady of irreproachable respectability. But surely a small draft of sensible sherry? 'Tis good for the blood and warming in winter."

The vicar's wife glanced down at the ladylike decanter and small, delicate glass on his tray, presented on a circle of lace. He'd outdone himself really, making it look as innocuous and feminine and respectable as possible. If he were a lady, he imagined he would find it nigh irresistible.

Mrs. Sarah Goodrich paused a little too long before shaking her head again in refusal.

Got you.

Jasper put on a heartbroken face. "Pray, do not force me to tell his lordship that his offering did not meet your standards."

Mrs. Vicar, as Jasper decided to call her in that moment, turned to him with her eyes wide. "Lord Matthias requested this? For me? Specifically?"

"But, of course!" Jasper lied, all in good cause. Besides, the gloved hand behind his back had his fingers firmly crossed. "His lordship knows perfectly well that a woman of your standing would never partake of champagne or any other decadent refreshment. That's why he sent for this particular sherry, as it is, er, fortified." Fortified by his lordship's smoothest whisky, that is. Jasper fluttered his eyelashes and tried to look as innocent as possible.

Yielding to temptation, Mrs. Vicar reached out for the tiny thimble-sized glass full of rich red liquid. "Well, I suppose it would be quite rude to turn down such a..."

"Respectable?"

"And generous offering." Mrs. Vicar took the glass and sipped the merest drop onto her lips to taste cautiously.

"I fear, like most medicinal drinks, it is best tossed back swiftly." Jasper delivered his entirely untrue advice with a note of deep regret. Surely he would be forgiven someday, after his plan came to fruition.

Mrs. Vicar took his advice and tossed back the whisky, ah, *sherry*, with swift determination.

Smoothly, Jasper took the tiny glass from her hand, refilled it and slipped it back between her gloved fingers before she had even a moment to analyze the taste.

"There now. Must drink up. It is good for you."

Mrs. Vicar looked down at her little glass in surprise. "Oh dear. Didn't I? Well."

Again the little red drink disappeared with surprising alacrity. Jasper was beginning to wonder if this was indeed Mrs. Vicar's first whisky.

Certainly she was nicely warmed up by now? He kept his tray still and shifted himself into a more intimately conversant position. "Truly, the staff here at Havensbeck is thrilled to have persons of your and your husband's stature as our guests this evening. Tell me, how does Haven's celebration compare to Green Dell's?"

"Well..."

After several minutes of highly informative comparison, Jasper realized he'd been quite correct. Behind Mrs. Vicar's chilly reserve lurked a good old-fashioned gossip. All she needed was a drop or three of sherry/whisky and an encouraging ear.

"And Miss Goodrich? How did you and the vicar come to be caretakers of the young lady and her brother? It is most admirable of you."

And she was off again.

Oh, yes. Mrs. Vicar was like a squirrel's winter cache, filled to bursting with excellent nuggets of information.

"Tell me more about young Simon."

SIMON GOODRICH WAS very good at not being noticed. When Bernie had a mind to give him a soaking in the bath, or when the Ladies League felt the need to grill him on his knowledge of the Good Book, he'd learned how to slip through rooms and doorways like a shadow. So when a well-intentioned adult had some improving activity in mind, Simon was always "just here a moment ago."

Tonight, he'd slipped past his departing family members to stow away in the boot space of the John Barton's cart. He'd never done such a thing before but it seemed like a good notion at the time. Eventually he'd wished he'd thought to bring a blanket to pad the hard wooden surface over the bumps, and maybe to snuggle in when the chill began to creep into the little box. However, all in all he was proud of his solution to his problem.

It wasn't fair that he couldn't attend the ball simply because he was eight. That was like a punishment just for not being big enough!

He hadn't had much trouble getting into the grand house either, for although the place was bustling with activity, the servants and guests were far too occupied to spot a silent child in the shadows. He even managed to slip into the dining room and filch a giant slice of cake to take into hiding with him.

Bernie had told him all about her tour of the house, especially when he'd pretended to have hurt feelings over not being included. Well, mostly pretended. So he knew that there was a place to sit up high and look down over the ballroom. He thought he might like that view, like a hawk watching the field.

He found it rather quickly, which was surely further proof that his mission was a righteous one. It was like a long, curved room in the shape of a new moon, with one wall missing, just a fancy railing there instead. He found himself all alone up there, with only a few rows of empty chairs facing outward. The expanded balcony was a darkened half-arc around the brilliant ballroom, opposite the grand entry stair. It was a grand view of the dance floor and although the shadows around him were a little spooky, the dimness made sure no one could see him peering between the railings of the balustrade, even if they looked up.

He settled in with his cake on his lap preparing to dig in, when a hustle and bustle on the far end of the mezzanine made him duck away from the railing around the grand ballroom into what seem to be a bit of a blind alley. Hidden in the shadows, he watched the sudden flurry of activity on the mezzanine with dismay.

A bunch of men in fancy suits entered by the same doorway Simon had used. They carried strange boxes into the open space of the mezzanine. That was when Simon realized what all those chairs were for. Oh, dash it all.

The men took musician's musical instruments out and began to plink and plunk at them. It didn't sound very nice at all, in Simon's opinion. A bit rickety-rackety and all over the place. He wouldn't want to dance to it, that was for certain!

He might as well sit down. It certainly looked as though the intruders were going to stay.

Simon grumbled in his dark corner and nibbled on his cake. The explosion of pastry and sugar and dried fruit in his mouth barely made up for his disappointment at losing his superior vantage point.

But after a while the strange discordant sounds became very nice. The music was really pretty. The chatter and bustle from below proved too much for his curiosity.

Hoping that the musicians were far too busy to look his way, since their eyes were fixed on their papers before them, Simon scooted out of his shadow and eased his way up to the balcony railing once more. He comforted himself that he was small and his clothes were dark and there were no candles at his end of the mezzanine. He knew that when one was right next to a candle, it was really hard to see the darkness beyond.

And then the sight below caught his attention. The chandeliers were all glowy with light and the dangling glassy bits made little shimmery lights dance all over the ballroom like fairies. Down below him, people sat or stood all around the edges, like a pie crust surrounding the swirling colorful dancers in the middle. It was pretty.

Simon had to force himself to finish his magnificent cake, but he drew on his strong character and his fortitude and persevered. Then he was terribly full. His belly stuck out and he felt like a stick that had eaten a pumpkin. He curled up on his side and pillowed his head on his arm and watched the marvelous whirling, glittering ballroom until his heavy eyelids fell shut.

WHEN HIS LORDSHIP led Bernie to an empty spot on the dance floor, which didn't take long because he was Lord Matthias and the seas parted before him, and pulled her closer, she went to him as if he were a magnet and she, nothing but a helpless lump of iron.

Suddenly it was Bernadette who felt awkward and shy. A few lessons long ago and an afternoon of waltzing with an eight-year-old had not come close to preparing her to dance in the arms of a handsome, titled man of accomplishment.

Although his hold was entirely appropriate for their newly acquainted relationship, he dipped his head closer to whisper in her ear. "If you allow me to lead, I believe I can get us to the end safely."

Oh heavens. Had she been leading? She bit at the corner of her lip as she grinned at him awkwardly. "I'm so sorry. I was teaching Simon today."

He pursed his lips slightly. "If you taught him to follow, there are going to be some very surprised ladies in a few years."

Bernie blushed. "Sweet Christmas Bells on a Stick!" she muttered under her breath. She was already making a muck of it!

Oh well, it was a good thing she had already given up on impressing him. Handsome, wealthy lords were on a shelf so high she could not reach it even on her tiptoes. She gave a slightly wistful sigh as she reminded herself that although she had very nice teeth, occasionally obedient hair, and a varied, if patchy, education, that a man like Lord Matthias would doubtless shop for a wife at glittering house parties and shimmering London balls.

With that, she tossed her girlish dreams into a closet and put a broom handle against the latch. She would *not* be silly Bernie tonight. *Bernadette* resolved to enjoy herself to the utmost. When this holiday was done, she would go back to Green Dell and chase chickens and dust hymnals and fish in her little pond. This greenery-draped hall might not be a shimmering London ballroom, but it was the closest she would ever see.

Silly Bernie began to fling herself most determinedly against that flimsy closet door. Cool, disinterested Bernadette was having a very difficult time holding it shut, especially when handsome, achingly gallant Lord Matthias swept her around so masterfully.

Oh heavens, this was bound to go badly for her.

If you are silly enough to fall in love with a lord, why not set your cap for a king? Why settle for a mortal man at all? The archangels are all handsome fellows, no doubt.

The scoffing voice in her head sounded rather too much like Aunt Sarah for Bernie's comfort.

Then again, this wasn't love. This was only a waltz.

Foolish girl.

In revolt against that irritatingly realistic voice, Bernie threw herself into the dance. Tossing shyness aside, she set out to prove that Mama had done her job well. When Lord Matthias lifted a brow at her success, she lifted her own in challenge.

His gaze narrowed in response. He then set out to impress her with his excellent lead, moving her about the floor with such authority that she felt as though her slippers floated above the marble. His hand was warm on her waist, his blue eyes were locked on hers and they moved together without effort or thought. The other dancers faded into a colorful blur and Bernie fancied that they were the only couple dancing in the entire world.

Unwilling to let him see the elation rising within her, Bernie tilted her head back to gaze up at the chandeliers above the ballroom until the little flames turned to stars in her vision. The swirling dance begun to feel as natural as breathing. His lordship's arms were strong and his gloved hands warm where they touched her.

Foolish, foolish girl.

I wish this dance would never end. She sighed in dreamy delight.

Was it her imagination or did his hands tighten on her ever so slightly? And then the music swelled once more into the early strains of the tune. Bernie blinked and looked at her partner in surprise. "Did I say that out loud?"

Lord Matthias was gazing at her intensely. Bernie felt abruptly shy again. She looked away, as if glancing at the other dancers. There were no other dancers. All the other guests were standing in a circle around them, pushed to the edges of the floor as if to give them as much room as possible. All eyes were on them.

Bernie felt a giggle rise. "Do not take alarm, my lord, but I believe we are being watched."

MATTHIAS HAD BEEN lost somewhere between counting the freckles that crested the top of her nose and trying to discern exactly how many colors of green mingled in her vivid eyes, while he tried to slow the pounding of his heart by reminding himself that she was just an ordinary country girl who would soon leave Havensbeck far behind.

At her warning, he tore his gaze away and stared over her head as they turned about the floor. His people were watching them, standing absolutely still with gazes riveted. He had the strangest feeling that they thought if they moved, they might frighten a wild thing away.

Is that wild thing me? Or her?

He stamped down the urge toward dignity and swept the

astonishing Miss Goodrich faster into the dance.

The crowd moved back in respect for their lord and then they did waltz alone in the center of the lovely hall of blue and gold, spangled by candlelight and crystal and something new, something that had not been in the world half an hour before.

As he spun her about once more, Bernie threw back her head and laughed aloud.

Chapter 12

MATTHIAS FALTERED IN the waltz step. His entire body forgot a dance he'd known since boyhood as his heart rose up and threatened to stop his breath.

Bernadette laughing in his arms.

Marianna laughing in his arms.

He felt odd and vulnerable and the ballroom was too bright and too loud.

I can't breathe.

His chest ached. His soul felt stretched between two points in time. The pounding in his head drowned out the musicians and the crowd and the voice of the young woman before him, asking what was the matter.

The past and the pain and the loss, his friends for so long, his only companions, pulled at him the way a band of brothers would tug one of their own away from a cliff's edge.

The future stretched out before him, beckoning him onward, tempting him with clear skies and far reaches, if only he would dare to jump. Fly.

Fall.

He stepped back. The past breathed a sigh of relief. He stepped back again and the future looked confused and stricken and so very disappointed. Her cheeks paled and she looked mortified.

Then his retreating feet carried him out of the ballroom and down the hallway that led deeper into the house. There, her portrait hung, facing him where the hallway split and turned.

Marianna.

Did her beautiful eyes accuse? Did her brow furrow at his faithlessness? Did she lift a hand to reach out to him, to stay his departure, to keep him at her side.

This Marianna was a thing of oil and canvas and memory, that was all. She did not speak, she did not touch.

She did not laugh, not anymore.

The past did not nourish. It did not sustain. Life went on without him. And he opened his hand and let that life slip right by him, turning instead to flee deeper into the darkness of his house, his haven, his never-changing shrine to all that was.

He could feel Marianna's eyes following him as he strode away. For the first time, it didn't feel particularly comforting. They were only paint, after all.

BERNIE STOOD ALONE in the center of the grand, luxurious ballroom and died a little inside.

She'd been so stupid, to read the words of a man writing to his lost love and to imagine for a moment that those words might have been for her.

His face. His eyes, full of confusion and pain, like a man fleeing darkness.

Fleeing her.

The murmurs of the ball guests pierced her awareness. Glancing around, she saw all faces turned her way, all eyes fixed upon her.

There were two directions to run. One was out, away from Havensbeck, away from the stunned audience, away from the dark, broken man who could scarcely look at her suddenly.

Or there was *in.*

Well, she'd followed him this far. Bernie picked up her skirts and ran after the lord of the manor.

When she left the ballroom, she saw a dark flutter down at the end of a long hallway. She stopped to pluck a candle from the nearest sconce, ignoring the splash of hot wax on her glove. Then she scurried down the hall. She thought she'd seen the flutter moving off to the right.

She turned and followed. Then she found herself face to face with the most beautiful woman she had ever seen. More lovely than Mama, even. Her mouth went dry.

The portrait hung just a bit higher so that the gaze of the stunning creature seemed to look right past Bernie, over her head as if she were of no importance whatsoever.

His letters had fallen short, Bernie realized. He'd never quite managed to communicate Marianna's porcelain perfection.

Was this why Jasper had distracted her with cattle thieves and lace smugglers, to keep her from seeing this vision?

Matthias's lady had been utterly dazzling. Flawless skin glowed even in paint and pigment. Rich brunette hair flowed over her shoulders and into the folds of her pale blue silk robe that brought out the flash of her laughing summer-sky blue eyes. Her rose-tinted lips curved in a small smile of endearing vulnerability.

And on Marianna's lap sat a tiny chubby boy, hardly more than two years old, with pink cherub cheeks, his mama's blue eyes and a great mop of his papa's ebony curls.

Simon.

Bernie's first thought was that her own skinny, shabby Simon had been that adorably plump once, with chubby baby fists and fleshy little toes like fat pink pearls.

Her second, rather more unworthy thought was that she was an idiot for thinking she could ever fill a void left by a woman like that.

And why should you wish to try? Aunt Sarah spoke in her mind. *Stop daydreaming, Bernadette. The blue-eyed beauty in that portrait has nothing to do with you.*

That was certainly true. Bernie was suddenly terribly afraid that this house and its lady and her heartbroken lord had not a thing at all to do with her.

And never would.

JOHN BARTON FOUND her as she slunk back through the ballroom, looking for her aunt and uncle. If only she could leave!

Bernie felt sick. She was an idiot. No one knew better than she how he still mourned his wife! *What did I think, that I was going to sail into his arms and make him forget his pain?*

Yes, that was exactly what she'd thought, reading his letters over and over again, hoarding them close, like talismans of a glittering future with the sort of man who loved with his whole heart.

But it wasn't whole. Not anymore. She knew that but she hadn't wanted to believe it. She was just a silly, stubborn girl, using up candle stubs to read words that were never, ever meant for her. She was a sneak-thief or possibly a fortune-hunter, except that the fortune she'd wanted was the noble, kind man himself, not his riches. Did that distinction matter, when she was here under false pretenses, behaving as if she were trying to make friends when she already knew him better than she knew anyone but Simon?

"Miss Goodrich! How are you enjoying the ball?"

Bernie pressed her eyes closed to squeeze back the incipient tears of mortification. Then she turned with the best smile she could muster. It wasn't much to speak of. "John."

The sturdy Vicar Barton didn't seem to notice. He grinned at her winningly, as if he'd finally found her after a long search.

"Yes, here I am."

His grin faltered slightly at her flat tone. She felt ashamed.

He was handsome and attentive and clearly eager for her company. Every word should not have to be hauled from her lips as if made of lead. Her smile should not be such a stingy thing for such a nice fellow.

I must do better. I will do better.

She assented to a dance, hoping it would give her a moment to gather her thoughts and not be such a dull stick.

By the time they'd circled the floor twice in a lively country dance, Bernie was feeling better. Action always helped clear her mind.

Perhaps it was all just a passing fancy. Surely she would forget it eventually. Thankfully, she'd never said anything about her silly hopes, not even to Simon. No one knew that she'd almost made the most terrific fool of herself.

And if it hurt to think of *him*—and she rather thought it would, likely for a long time—then it would hurt. She'd seen enough of the world, enough of true pain, to know that she would survive her infatuation. Even recover from it, eventually. Perhaps.

With her thoughts turned so inward, she was not entirely aware of dancing. Therefore, she did very well at it. When the music ended and she turned one last circle back into John Barton's embrace, she was startled by the bright sparkle in his eyes as he gazed down at her.

Christmas Bells, he was handsome!

Well, at least that part of her still worked. She smiled back a little more naturally, relieved by the notion that she perhaps was not too terribly shattered if she could still enjoy the sight of an impressive fellow beaming at her.

His expression brightened further at her smile. "Come, let us find somewhere to talk."

"Oh." She cast a wistful glance back at the dance floor. She'd only just begun to enjoy herself a bit. "Yes, of course."

"Somewhere to talk" turned out to be in an unpopulated corner behind the refreshment table, half-hidden by a potted palm. Bernie waited while John fetched a glass of lemonade for her. Some of the older women were partaking of something stronger. Even Aunt Sarah had a thimble-sized glass of sherry.

Bernie had tasted champagne once, at another Christmas party, a long time ago. Her mother had handed her the glass for a moment while she'd adjusted the wide silk bow on thirteen-year-old Bernie's head. Bernie had sneaked a tiny sip of bubbles and forbidden mature indulgence. She'd liked it very much.

However, lemonade was very nice too. There were no lemons in Green Dell, no hothouses with tiny pruned trees in pots, drooping with the weight of ripe lemons in midwinter. She had no idea where she'd seen that, but it came back to her as she tasted the bright, tart drink.

Perhaps it was experiencing a bit more of the world that was bringing such memories back. Green Dell never changed. The old, crumbling vicarage never changed, except to become more damaged and difficult to maintain. The days were all the same, full of work and service and, for everyone but Simon, worry. Lean but heartfelt Christmases came and went, the turn of year after year.

John was speaking. Bernie blinked and fought hard to catch up.

"This is a very plum assignment, I'm told. I'm afraid I always pictured myself somewhere a bit more rustic, I suppose. I thought I might be of greater good to a place of greater need."

He would, she thought. An intelligent, vigorous fellow like John could do so much fine work in the world.

He went on. "But I had a good reason for taking this particular post."

Bernie looked up at his pause and saw him looking at her closely. *Stop woolgathering and pay attention to the man who actually does want to talk to you!* When he waited for a response, she nodded. "And what is your reason?"

He leaned close. "*You,* Bernadette. You are my reason—for *everything.*"

THE LEMONADE SUDDENLY seemed to sour in Bernie's mouth. She was forced to swallow before she was quite prepared. Her throat burned and she realized she wasn't breathing properly. She pressed her palm to her throat and wheezed out, "What did you say?

"I invited your family here for a reason." His focus on her was intense, absolute and undivided. "I aim to beg your uncle for your hand in marriage. If you say you want me as a husband.

"Husband?" Bernie squeaked. She stared at him.

He gave an awkward half-smile. "It must mean something that you have no words, for I thought you had something to say about every little thing on earth. I only hope that it means something encouraging."

She shut her mouth, for it was doing absolutely no good hanging open like a chicken-coop door. Breathing might help. She inhaled deeply, calmly, then burst out, "But we just met! Again."

Something sparked in John's clear, untroubled gray eyes that frightened her or possibly thrilled her. It was just so hard to tell!

He stepped a little closer and took her hand in both of his. "Bernadette Goodrich, I have known you—and liked you very well—for six years. I remember the first time I saw you, when your uncle and I greeted you and Simon at the coaching inn downriver. There was a governess with you, seeing you into the hands of family. I don't recall her name. You were so pale and sad, sitting up so straight in your uncle's cart, riding back to Green Dell clutching fat, baby Simon sleeping on your lap. I ached for you."

His tone softened with pity. "I thought you were pretty, of course, but it was as I watched you make your way in a new place that I came to admire you. I knew perfectly well that your life before was very different, but you tried so hard to master everything you could to take the burden from your aunt. You turned your hand to work that you could not possibly have imagined yourself doing and you persisted until you accomplished everything. And you made sure that little Simon laughed and played and felt safe, even when anyone could see that your heart was broken."

Bernie had to drop her gaze then, for he'd clearly seen so much more than she'd ever known. She looked at his large hands, wrapped around her one. Those hands, she had to admit, felt exceedingly warm and secure holding hers.

He went on. "You were too young and I was too soon into my studies for anything to come of it then. I thought that if I waited, and if I found just the right position, that I would be enough of a prize to catch your interest."

At that she looked up, startled. "You waited? For me?"

At her continued disbelief, he seemed to falter. "I thought, well, your uncle wrote to me often, and I to him. In every letter, he devoted much of it to you. How proud he was of you, or something clever you'd said to make him laugh, and how he worried for your future when he could no longer provide for you. He said you liked hearing of me as well." He swallowed then and blinked. "It only now occurs to me that it might have been a bit of wishful thinking on his part. Or mine."

Bernie recalled her uncle reading John's letters before the fire, sharing news of him with them all. And she had liked it, very much. Now that she thought about it, she'd had a few wondering thoughts about him as well.

Until the winter day when she'd found the first bottle in the river.

Her throat tightened further. She'd been so foolish! Such a silly, romantic dreamer! Here John had been, waiting for her, working for her, while she'd been mooning over a grief-stricken stranger who'd not even known she'd existed until a few days ago.

Now, she frowned up at the man who had just offered her everything any woman might dream of: a fine home, a good heart, a handsome exterior and what seemed like true devotion. *Am I his Marianna?*

Her mouth opened. What was she to tell him? Shame brought on a flush. "I have absolutely no notion of what to tell you."

He flinched a little at that, then gave a rueful bark of laughter. "Your honesty only endears you to me more, Bernadette. Confusion, I can understand. And I much prefer candid bewilderment to polite hints of false hope. You did not turn and run away. Might I deduce from that encouraging fact that the notion is not entirely distasteful to you?"

"No. I mean, yes." She had to laugh at herself then, a gulping, panicky sound. "I'm sorry. I am confounded. I confess that I did think of you, of us, at one time." She looked away. "But I seem to have given up on that aspiration."

He nodded and sighed. "I left it too long. I know. You are twenty already. Everything just took longer than I'd hoped. I wanted just the right position, just the right place." He waved his hand around the ballroom.

Bernie knew that he meant the village of Haven, not the manor, but she cringed inside. Not this place, not for her. But that pretty village? And that gracious vicarage?

He went on in a rush. "I do not wish to plead a lost cause, but I have so much to tell you about Haven. One of the reasons I chose it is that the school is very good. Just the thing for an enquiring lad. Or we could speak to his lordship about tutors."

Mortification squirmed in her belly. *Oh, no. Not a word about his lordship. Not right now.* Bernie held out a hand to stop John's torrent of words. "There is no need to convince me that Haven is a fine place, John. Or that you have much to offer any woman."

She took a breath. She was not a liar, but she could not bear to expose her foolishness to this excellent man. "It is only that I didn't realize. I truly had no idea you still thought of me. I thought you'd gone away, never to return. I thought I knew my future, caring for my family."

"And then I fling my heart into your hands without warning." He shook his head. "I understand. I have spoken my piece. I will not pester you with it, dear Bernadette." He brushed a strand of hair from her cheek with a gentle fingertip. "When you've thought it through, you know where to find me."

Yes, she thought. Just down the lane from the inn.

In that fine vicarage, with a good village school nearby.

Chapter 13

THE CARRIAGE BUMPED a bit on the snow-packed lane, but Bernie could not tear her gaze from Aunt Sarah's face. "You want me to wed John Barton?"

"Well, why not?" Aunt Sarah folded her arms before her, a bit defensively to Bernie's view. "He's a fine, established man, a good man! It's a worthy match. You'll make a good vicar's wife, eventually."

"Now, now, Sarah. Give the girl a moment to absorb the notion." Uncle Isaiah turned to Bernie, his kind eyes sympathetic. "Just think about it, Bernie, dear. John is in need of a wife and you two seem to get on well. And," he shrugged a bit helplessly, "we *know* John."

Know John? What did that mean, precisely? "Get on? We danced one dance! We went for a half hour's walk! I'm supposed to base such a monumental decision on a reel, three fields and a badger's burrow?"

"You're too old to think like a romantic child," Aunt Sarah muttered with a sniff. "You have no idea how hard a world this can be for a woman!"

Bernie gazed across the carriage at Sarah's bent shoulders and roughened hands. *Oh, I have a fairly good notion.* She felt her face grow hot with shame. She'd seen more than her aunt realized in the lives of the villagers. Girls disgraced and rushed into bad matches, too young. Older spinsters living on charity and the pickings of ever more meager gardens as their strength failed them.

There were far more terrible fates for a woman than to marry a good man and live in a fine, modern vicarage. She and John likely *would* get on. They would work for the village and perhaps have some children and spend their entire lives together, getting on.

She wanted more.

I'm so blasted selfish I can't stand myself right now. But I still want more.

Even now, in the carriage, she saw her aunt fussing over her uncle, who was visibly drooping. Suddenly, she realized why they were pushing her for a match with Vicar Barton. Isaiah Goodrich was old and weary, and Aunt Sarah was worn to the bone. The post was too hard, the village of Green Dell in too much need, but the vicar couldn't retire. If they could scarcely survive on the vicar's income, the pension would never care for all four of them.

I've been so blind.

Two orphans at their door had meant a significant dent in the couple's ability to stretch a vicar's income, yet Bernie had not realized that for a long time. They had never said a word to her about it. She'd had to overhear a quietly worried conversation when she'd needed to visit the privy one late night.

That was the summer she'd built the dam, dragging the stones on a ragged horse blanket she'd tied around her shoulders like a cape. She'd found a book in her uncle's library about stone work and had done her sixteen-year-old best. When the first dam had washed out during the spring rains, she'd done it again, twice as wide with portals built in to let high waters pass.

Carefully, she folded her hands before her. This was like the dam, wasn't it? Something that would help her aunt and uncle, and Simon, too. Something that only she could do.

A vicar's wife. A life of gravity and dedication. Bernie lifted her gaze to her aunt across from her. Sarah may be work worn and hard-edged, but in her way, she seemed content. She doted on her husband and the two of them were strong partners, shepherds and examples to all.

There were worse fates, to be sure.

No more silly fancies about broken-hearted lords sweeping in to rescue her. *You could help everyone in your family, if you would simply grow up.*

Yes. Rebellion was for children. She could take this next step. After all, she was smart and strong and she understood what a vicar's life entailed.

"You're right, Uncle Isaiah. I'll give it a good thinking over, I promise."

They nodded, pleased. Still, a tiny voice in Bernie's mind wailed, *But why must it be Haven?*

MATTHIAS LURKED IN the recesses of Havensbeck Manor until the last of the guests had either departed or taken to one of the bedchambers prepared for them. How could he face anyone after that strange and public moment of near-lunacy?

Really, there is only one person you cannot face.

He would have to, at some point. He'd behaved like a lout, throwing her aside in the middle of a waltz!

What must she think of him?

What would Marianna think of him?

Divided loyalties tore more powerfully than hungry wolves, it seemed. Matthias felt bloodied and defenseless between them.

Beautiful, exhilarating Marianna, the starry-eyed memory of life-past, the spellbinding passion of his youth, the woman he'd adored beyond sense, the mother of his beloved Simon.

Versus cheerful and compassionate Bernadette who, entirely without mystery or wile, had managed to laughingly stir him from his graveside slumber, exhaling the sweet breath of the lively present to warm his numbed cheeks. She even had a Simon of her own in tow.

There was comfort in the known. Turning his face back into the past, he could simply go on as he had been. He could do his duty, he could perform mostly as a normal man, except for a few weeks every winter when his grip on normality would slip and he would drink far too much and write letters to the dead. The year would pass much as any one before it. And so would the year after that, and the year after that.

The stirring of emotions long banked in the smoke-stained depths of his soul bid fair to upsetting that endless chain of mere existence. Bernadette came, like a practical housewife with a broom, and threatened to sweep the ashes of his heart into her keeping.

Restless, unable to remain still, Matthias began to stride the empty night halls of his manor, his gut feeling like ashes swirling before the force of a broom.

The simile spooled onward, until he pictured pretty, grinning Miss Bernadette Goodrich smacking the dust from the carpets of his spirit, polishing the patina from his once sparkling mind, throwing open his heavy draperies and calling forth the sunlight to wake him every morning, and curling close and warm with him every night.

Ahem.(Why did the voice sound so much like Jasper?) *Perhaps you ought to first make her your lady wife?*

Wife?

Marry?

I am already married.

No, you are not.

Oh. He'd forgotten again. The vows he'd made that day had expired, like a lease, the title of husband torn from him.

Father, as well? He paced faster, taking a turn above the ballroom, seeking scope for longer strides as if he could outpace his own battling emotions.

No. He'd had a son. The mere two years allotted made no difference to the way his child had changed his heart. He would always be Simon's father, until the day he died.

Funny, bright-souled Simon!

The bundle of bulky jacket and awkward boots lay heaped at Matthias's feet where he'd stopped half-around the mezzanine above the dark ballroom. The bundle snored lightly.

"Simon?"

THE CARRIAGE RIDE back to the inn seemed to take forever. Surely, Bernie thought, she could have walked the distance faster on her own!

Of course, she wasn't on her own. Uncle Isaiah was pale with exhaustion and even Aunt Sarah flagged badly. Bernie had to help them to their chamber, and then stayed to build up their fire despite Aunt Sarah's weak protestations of wastefulness.

As she fluffed up her uncle's pillows and kissed the top of his balding head goodnight, he took her hand in his chill, dry one.

"We only want you to be cared for properly," he said sadly.

Bernie extracted her hand with a gentle pat. "I know that."

It was all perfectly sensible. Fortunate, even. John cared for her, and looked forward to caring for Simon. She was the lucky one.

"I cannot come to an answer until I speak to Simon," she said quietly.

Aunt Sarah bristled. "I can't think why! It isn't up to a little boy!"

Uncle Isaiah put a hand on Sarah's arm. "You do that, Bernie. Go on now. I'm sure he's still wide awake, waiting to hear all about the ball."

Aunt Sarah fussed again, albeit half-heartedly, as Bernie and Uncle Isaiah shared a look of understanding. Then Bernie turned and picked up her skirts to make her way up the stairs.

But the chamber she shared with Simon was dark. He must have been more exhausted by his adventures than she'd thought, for there was only a lump beneath the covers barely visible in the glow from the coals.

She didn't want to wait until morning, not when she was feeling rather determined and self-sacrificing now. Better to put this matter to rest before she weakened.

Sitting down on the mattress next to her dearest little lump, she reached to pull down the coverlet.

Then she leaped to her feet and ran back down the hall. When she burst into their chamber, Aunt Sarah and Uncle Isaiah looked up in surprise.

"He's gone!"

MATTHIAS KNELT NEXT to Simon, curled sound asleep in the mezzanine. There was a smear of cream on his upper lip.

Matthias had missed out on the cake, due to the ill effects of his own uncertainties. Served him right, of course. Still, he had once liked cake.

Despite Matthias's gentle prodding, there was no waking young Master Goodrich from his sweets-sodden nap. Matthias gave up on that idea and lifted the little boy into his arms instead, grubby boots and all. Simon stirred slightly, wiggling into Matthias's arms. He let out a great sigh of satisfaction.

"I like it here." Simon yawned with the abandon of the very young and very sleepy. He went on in a drowsy murmur. "We had a big house once. I remember. Everyone thinks I don't, but I do."

Then there was silence except for the thudding of Matthias's pulse in his ears. He'd carried his own child like this, limp-tired and boneless, cradled against his heart.

Matthias was entirely surprised to find that he didn't feel pain at this reminder. He felt warm and necessary in a way that being lord of the manor had never made him feel. It was wonderful to pick up a sleepy child and tuck him against his shoulder. It felt right.

There could be more children in his life, if he chose. Becoming a father again would cost his own Simon nothing. As he passed Marianna's portrait in the hallway, Matthias stopped to look into her smiling eyes once more.

You're being very silly, Mattie, he could hear her say the way she used to, with a depth of fondness in her amusement that belied her teasing tone. It occurred to him that of all the people in the world, his lovely Marianna would be the first to scold him for wasting all his love on the dead.

In his study, he balanced Simon Goodrich's slight weight easily with one arm while he reached out to tug on the smaller bell-pull hidden behind the other, the one that called Jasper and Jasper alone.

It was time for a certain little boy to be off in his own bed at the inn, and time for Matthias to face Miss Bernadette Goodrich with his heartfelt apology in hand. Perhaps bringing back her brother might ease her indignation?

Matthias could not imagine sunny Bernadette becoming indignant. Still, he'd wager she looked very pretty when cross.

THE NIGHT WAS stark black, as dark as any night Bernie had ever seen. The thick covering of crystalline snow helped reflect back the searchers' lanterns only a little before the circles of light waned to shadow and then to nothingness.

Bernie scarcely felt the cold for her terror for Simon, although she was happy she had managed to persuade Uncle Isaiah to remain behind. Her aunt and uncle were far too fragile for such a venture. Secretly, Bernie was glad enough to be able to surge ahead as quickly as her own weary legs could take her. She'd borrowed Uncle's boots and thrown on as many layers of woolens as she could but still she shivered in her old coat and scarf.

The low temperatures only drove her fear higher. Simon was so small and thin and she was certain he'd been too foolish to dress himself properly. She ought to have simply allowed him to go to the ball or at least to go down to the inn public room to join some of the other village children who were spending the evening there. But he'd looked so ragged this morning, with his large eyes shadowed and his thin cheeks so pale. He'd told her that he was all right, but Bernie could not squelch the memory of him spinning away from her on his pitiful raft of ice. All she'd wanted was to wrap him in cotton wool and tuck him away, safe and sound for just a little while....

A little while so you could dance in the arms of his lordship?

Bernie refused to waste one instant of her stamina on self-recrimination. There would be plenty of time for that later. The only thing that mattered now was finding Simon. She rushed ahead of the innkeeper and the other village man who walked with her. She strained forward like a hound on a leash, searching her soul and her senses for any inkling of Simon's location. Surely she should be able to sense him if he were near!

She was so panicked and fear-stricken that she was not making sense anymore. She knew it, and she cared not at all.

She had her own small lantern so she did not notice that she left her companions behind until it was too late, and she had lost sight of any other bobbing lights other than her own. It was disconcerting but not alarming, not for her own sake. She knew where she was, more or less. The valley was a valley, just like her own, after all. The ground sloped down to the river and up to the hills and the river flowed from the village southward and westward. That helped somewhat in that she knew that she would be able to find her way either to the village or to the manor. It did not help her find Simon.

She slogged onward wearily picking her feet up high and stomping them down again to work her way through the knee-deep snow. Every once in a while she stopped to catch her breath and to call Simon's name. "Simon! *Simon!*"

After perhaps a dozen repetitions of this she heard a sound in reply.

"Hello, there!"

"Simon?" The voice had been deep. Bernie swung around in confusion. "Where are you?" She held the lantern high. "Simon?"

"Bernie-Bernie-Bernie!"

Chapter 14

B ERNIE GASPED, HER heart stuttering in the most profound relief she'd ever felt. *"Simon!"* She grabbed up her skirts and lunged as fast as she could in the direction of that cry. Her lantern swung wildly with her ragged progress so that when the black horse emerged from the shadows of the stark trees she didn't see it until it was almost upon her.

"Bernie-Bernie-Bernie!"

Bernie yelped, slipped and then sat down on her bottom in the snow. Barely keeping her lantern high with one hand she looked up, and up, *and up* the tall midnight shadow of horse until she saw Simon's dear, pointy little face staring at her from a circle of what must've been a half-dozen blankets wrapping him about.

"Oh! Simon! You're safe! Oh, you little--" She trailed off as her gaze continued to rise higher still to meet the handsome, shadowed eyes of Lord Matthias. "--*brother*," She blurted.

She wasn't wrong about the quirk of Lord Matthias's lips as she hastily replaced the word she'd been about to use. She suddenly became aware of her undignified sprawl in the snow, where she must indeed look like a flour sack in boots! She scrambled up in a clumsy fashion and stumbled toward the great dark horse.

Perseus did not seem inclined to welcome this strange bulky creature with the startling, swinging little lantern and the clomping, pitching step. He lifted his head in a temperamental fashion and uttered a horsey sound of anxiety.

"Settle down, you *brother*." Lord Matthias growled at his mount.

Bernie was far too overjoyed to care if she was being teased. She ran directly up to the nervous horse and began patting her free hand over Simon's bulky blanket cocoon.

"Are you *all right*? Where did you *go*? What were you *thinking*? How could you *do* this to me? Where did you find him?"

The last was directed at Lord Matthias, and she fixed him with an urgent stare. Lord Matthias blinked and swallowed. "Well, I found him in the mezzanine with an empty cake plate, taking a nap."

Simon looked upward at his rescuer in dismay. "You told!"

Lord Matthias looked back down at Simon. "Yes. I did. She does that to me."

"Me, too." Simon sighed. "I guess I just hoped maybe I'd grow out of it someday."

Bernie, finally satisfied that beneath his ridiculous bundling Simon was all in one piece, stepped back slightly from the restive Perseus and released a long sigh. She didn't mean to make it sound so weary and long-suffering, but honestly, she was weary and terribly tired of suffering!

"I thank you very much, my lord. I cannot believe Simon was so thoughtless as to put you to all this trouble." She slid a meaningful glare Simon's direction. He snuggled deeper into his safety of Lord Matthias's care, lifting the blanket up to cover most of his face except for his large, worried eyes.

"I'm sorry, Bernie. I just wanted to *see!*"

Bernie shook her head. "I understand, beastie. I wanted to see as well."

Lord Matthias began to peel some of the blankets away from Simon and Bernie realize that he meant to get down from his horse. "Oh no, my lord. Please ride on with Simon to the inn, if you will. My aunt and uncle are so worried."

Lord Matthias did not listen. He dismounted after fixing Simon's grip on the saddle, although Bernie noticed that he kept Perseus's reins in his own hands. Lord Matthias rounded on Bernie. "And leave you to wander around in the woods in the dark? On Christmas Eve?"

Now that Bernie heard him say it like that, she realized how silly she was being. She inhaled slowly. "Yes." She gathered her panic-tattered manners. "Thank you, my lord. I would very much appreciate your assistance back to the inn, for myself as well as my brother."

Bernie dearly hoped he did not mean to take them both back to the manor, instead. She hadn't crossed the river yet, so surely the village was closer. The last thing she wanted to do was to return to the site of her vast humiliation.

Lord Matthias bowed slightly and held out a hand for the lantern. Bernie gave it to him and he attached it in some mysterious way to the side of Perseus's saddle. Then he held out one hand to Bernie.

There was no help for it. Bernie was going to have to let him put her in the saddle. It wasn't possible for her to get up that gigantic horse on her own. And that mean that they would have to be very, very close together when he did so. And that was going to be rather too much like the dreadful waltz where he had practically fled from her presence.

Then she was in the saddle. It had been quite mercifully quick, yet her breath had stopped at the feel of his strong hands about her waist and the way that he so lightly tossed her aboard when she knew perfectly well that she was no dainty reed.

But her little bundled-up beastie was right there in her arms and she wrapped him close and tight, closing her eyes and lowering her face to the top of his rotten, disobedient little head. She gave him a little shake which he probably couldn't even feel through the many layers of quilts wrapped around him. "You're going to clean all the fish. Forever. Just so you know."

"Aw, Bernie." Still he leaned trustingly back against her, snuggled in right where he belonged.

Lord Matthias began retracing Bernie's steps, sensibly using her broken trail to ease his own path through the snow. For several long moments it was enough to feel the relief of Simon safe in her arms and also the relief of not having to walk all that way back in the snow, by herself, in the dark. What was it about being rescued that made one like someone despite all previous strange and unpleasant behavior?

Except that he hadn't been unpleasant. She'd already known how he felt about his former wife. She'd read those letters so very many times. It was her own fault for thinking that she could ever gain the attention of such a man when she knew perfectly well that his heart belonged to someone else.

All that dark confusion and pain in his face had been her fault. And the way his grief had overwhelmed him and the way he looked around at the crowd of his own people, who loved and revered him, as if surrounded by a pack of wolves? Her fault.

Well, she knew precisely how he felt, didn't she? She remembered the way normal sounds had startled her like thunder, and ordinary lights had stabbed her eyes. She recalled clearly how every sense had become as raw and naked as her battered soul in a world where nothing made sense the way it had before.

"It can overcome you that way," she said, just loud enough to be heard over the horse's snow-muffled tread. "It can carry you off like a flood, and there's nothing you can do about it until it passes."

Lord Matthias stopped in his forward march. He didn't turn but stood still for a long moment. It seemed as if there were no noise at all except for the creak of the saddle as Perseus shifted and his waffling breath as he nosed his master's collar in a horsey question. The midnight forest around them was as silent as the grave.

"I do not deserve your understanding." The words are hardly more than a whisper but Bernie heard them clearly.

She shook her head, although she knew he could not see her. "Of course you do. It is, after all, perfectly understandable."

He turned his head so that she could see his slanting cheekbone and strong jaw in the lantern's meager light.

"How is it that you can see so deeply within me?" His tone had gone husky and urgent. "How is it that you can see more clearly than I can see myself? What is this strange connection, Miss Goodrich? I have spoken to other people who have lost a loved one. Never have I experienced such true understanding with any of them."

Oh. Bernadette swallowed hard. In that moment she understood two things very clearly; one was the depth of her own foolishness and willful disregard for another's privacy and her entire culpability in upsetting and confusing this good man, and the other was that it was time to stop doing that. She'd been silly, and grasping, and ludicrously self-involved. She could not bear the pain she's caused in him.

For I love him so.

That hurt, oh heavens, how it *hurt*. To know it now? It was nothing like her obsession with her imaginary author of the letters. The force of that knowledge ached, and burned, and very nearly sickened her with the thoughtless damage she had done. Done by not realizing that her winter storyteller was a real man whose lovely wife and dearest child had died and left a great torn and aching hole where his heart should've been.

He was kind, and wonderful, and the lord of the manor, a man so far out of her reach that she should be shipped off to Bedlam immediately for even wishing he wasn't. She was in love with him, the real Matthias, not the fantasy.

Let him go. Let it all go.

She knew how. She had done it before, sending her mourning on its way so she could be the sister Simon needed.

So *because* she loved him, she must tell him the worst possible thing of all.

"Lord Matthias, we have no special connection," she said quietly. "I am not the person you think I am. Although I did not intend to be, it seems that I am a liar and something of a cheat. For I come from Green Dell, which lies a few miles downriver from Havensbeck. And for several years now, every year at Christmastime, I have fished a bottle or three or five from the river."

She saw him jerk slightly at her words and heard his long indrawn breath. She couldn't stop there. He deserved to know everything. "I have read your letters so many time I think I may know you better than anyone does, with the possible exception of Jasper. And although I hardly realized it myself, it seems that I have made myself privy to your deepest pain, which I have most surely used to gain far more of your attention than I deserve."

He didn't turn. He merely walked onward, leading Perseus through the snow. She was glad, for she was a coward indeed. In the circle of her arms she felt Simon jerk and lift his face toward her, but she squeezed him and shook her head, signaling him to be silent.

SHE KNEW *EVERYTHING*. Matthias kept his silence for quite a while after Miss Goodrich's revelation. It made him feel rather peculiar to think that she'd read his letters to Marianna and Simon. He tried to distill his exact opinion of that.

Should he be angry? At what, truly? It wasn't as if she'd climbed in his study window like a sneak-thief and pried open the drawers of his desk to find them. She had not taken anything from him that he had not freely tossed into the river himself.

He was astonished at himself for never having considered that an actual living person might lay hands upon the bottles and read their contents. He could possibly excuse himself by claiming to believe the bottles would smash upon the rocks downriver, and the waters wash the ink from the pages. That would be a very handy defense, yet he had never given it a single thought at all. It had been the only expression he could make of his grief and so he had done it again and again, although it had never done more than temporarily ease his agony.

The fact remained that the bottles had washed up, presumably at Miss Goodrich's very feet, and she had, as anyone would, extracted the letters and read them.

Then he did have a troubling thought. He stopped again and, without turning, asked, "Did you show my letters to anyone else?"

She hesitated, then answered. "I did. One person."

Her aunt, presumably. Or perhaps the vicar?

"I read them," Simon blurted behind him.

Matthias tilted his head. "You let a *child* read them?"

"My lord, when the letters first came I was but sixteen. I should hope you would excuse a young girl from sharing such a curiosity with her little brother."

Matthias nodded. That did seem reasonable. He began to walk again, his boots taking on more wet than he would like. His step grew heavy. It was very cold. Simon was quite thoroughly bundled, but Miss Goodrich was not.

"Is it much farther, my lord?" Bernadette's voice sounded strained and very quiet. Yes, she would be cold now that she was no longer stomping her way through the snow, charging about in the dark alone. Contrary creature.

It was as he had begun to suspect. She was quite mad, particularly on the topic of her little brother.

"It's not much farther now." He was correct. Soon they crested a small rise where they could see lights before them like a chain of diamonds down the road through the village. At that moment, a soft snowfall began. The feathery flakes shimmered in the light cast from the village windows. It was lovely. Simon made a noise of appreciation but Matthias said nothing more as they continued.

Perseus, sensing shelter and possibly oats, began to pick up the pace and Matthias walked faster as well. It was time to get these two into the warm inn.

"Are you feeling well enough?" he asked Miss Goodrich as they left the wood behind them and began to make their way down the village lane.

"Fairly so, my lord," she replied, her tone thoughtful. "It was rather painful to admit out loud to what I have done. However, I do feel much lighter by the telling of it."

Matthias felt the corners of his mouth quirk slightly. "I meant, are you warm enough?"

"Oh yes, my lord. Perseus is a most satisfactory source of heat."

Matthias walked them straight to the inn, for he knew the elder Goodriches would be beside themselves with worry. The stable-hand came running as Matthias was helping Miss Goodrich slip off the horse. The boy took the reins and then Bernadette's aunt and uncle emerged and converged on Simon. Matthias handed the child to his Uncle Isaiah while his Aunt Sarah fluttered over him very crossly indeed, which Matthias suspected hid her extreme happiness at his well-being.

Their attention temporarily on the little boy, Matthias turned to Bernadette and gazed down at her. She looked back at him. Her gaze was level and somber, but by no means crushed by their conversation and her confession.

Matthias exhaled slowly. "I am not angry at you for reading the letters. I am the one who threw them into the waters. I should not be surprised that they were found. I am glad they were read by someone who understands."

She folded her arms and hunched her shoulders slightly against the chill but her gaze never left his. "I shall not presume upon our unfair intimacy any further, but for one thing. You need not stay lost, my lord. I know it is hard, but you must concentrate on all the best things, like the people who smile at you, and the music and the children." She waved a hand at the sky, and then went on in a rush, as if she had to get the words out before he fled her. "And a perfect snowfall on Christmas Eve! There will come a day when your world will seem just a bit brighter, and brighter still the day after that. You should know that the people who are gone want you to enjoy the life still left to you. If I passed, I should be furious with Simon if he insisted on living his life in the shadow of my death!"

This was not comfort. This was criticism. No, not comfortable at all. Matthias shook his head, "I don't know what to do with you. You dismay and alarm me, Miss Goodrich."

Over the shoulder of his uncle, who was even then carrying him into the door of the inn, Simon lifted his head sleepily. "She does that to everyone."

Miss Goodrich continued to look him in the eye. "I even alarm myself sometimes." Then she smiled at him and he felt his pulse stutter again. "Now, I must thank you for saving my Simon, once again."

She went up on tiptoe to kiss his cheek. Without even realizing he did so, Matthias turned his head to catch her lips in his. *What am I doing?*

Her lips were cold but giving. Sweet, soft and full of life. No still and silent painting here. She stayed there on tiptoe for the length of a breath. Matthias dared not press the kiss further. She did not draw away.

When she dropped slowly back onto her heels, her smile was gone and no laughter remained in her wide gaze. Instead, her eyes shone strangely in the dim light of the inn lantern.

Were those *tears?* Why?

Before he could ask, she stepped back once, turned abruptly, then ran quickly into the inn without looking back at him again.

Matthias stood there in the cold night. The village grew darker by the moment as people, no doubt hearing that the missing child was safe home, begin to settle back down for the long winter's night. Finally even the lanterns in the public room of the inn were snuffed out. Matthias was alone in the inn-yard. The stable boy had taken Perseus to the stable so Matthias walked slowly into that warm and horsey structure.

In his borrowed stall, Perseus was still saddled but his bridle had been removed to allow him to enjoy his reward of a handful of oats. Matthias crossed his arms on the top railing of the stall and dropped his chin upon them.

"Now I am entirely confounded," he informed Perseus. Perseus shook his head and then lipped tenderly at Matthias's hair. This was less helpful than one might imagine.

Chapter 15

B ERNIE DID NOT consult with her brother after all. Last night's humiliating, albeit freeing, confession had proved to her precisely how nonsensical she had been. She was a grown woman. She would make the best decision for both of them.

The kiss had no bearing on anything at all. An accidental thing, or perhaps a bit of curiosity, but Lord Matthias was in love with another woman and always would be.

As for Simon, he liked John Barton. Of course, it went without saying that John would be very good to Simon. Bernadette had been holding her little brother up as some sort of shield before the difficulty of making such a life-altering decision. Again, very childish.

So that morning she roused her brother, dressed him quickly and sensibly and sent him down to breakfast without her. Then she sat before the vanity and took great care with her appearance. Almost as much as she had taken preparing for the ball on the night before. She pulled her hair back into a practical knot at the back of her neck. She put on her best everyday dress, the blue one. She even remembered to pinch her pale cheeks to bring a bit of color.

This is an excellent step forward. This is not an execution. A fine man awaits you downstairs and you are a very fortunate woman to have such a man ask for your hand.

She felt quite calm. The frantic stretching at the seams of her life had been quelled by the shame she felt over her ill-fated obsession with Lord Matthias. That last burst of extremely silly behavior at the ball had come none too soon. She did not despise herself for dreaming of the love of such a man. She only berated herself for mistaking such a dream for reality.

Appropriately dressed, entirely composed, she left the room with quick, even steps and descended the stair to join the family at breakfast. John already sat at the table with Aunt Sarah, Uncle Isaiah and Simon. While Bernadette watched, John bent low to say something to Simon. Simon laughed. Then John mussed Simon's hair and laughed as well. Aunt Sarah looked on benignly, as if she'd never scolded either Bernie or Simon for toying with their hair at the table. Uncle Isaiah looked on benevolently, the proud patriarch at ease.

This is my family now.

This is my future.

Bernadette, and yes, she was *Bernadette* now, moved to stand behind the last chair at the table. Isaiah and John rose to their feet in welcome. She smiled and waved them back.

"Happy Christmas, Uncle Isaiah, Aunt Sarah, Simon!" She turned her new, calm, mature smile on the man who gazed at her with growing hope in his eyes. "Happy Christmas, John. I should like to accept your very kind offer, if you still wish it so."

John beamed. Uncle Isaiah beamed. Aunt Sarah beamed. Simon looked quizzical and then resigned as understanding came clear.

Bernadette smiled firmly at her family. *Yes.* Such a little word, to bring such happiness to the people she loved.

John stood and rounded the table. "I cannot express my joy at your words! Happy Christmas, dear Bernie!" He took her into his arms. They were strong arms, welcoming arms.

They simply felt like the wrong ones.

Yet, what did it matter if deep down she felt as shattered as the ice on the edge of the rushing River Churnet?

Surely winter could not last forever, could it?

IN THE NEW-FALLEN morning snow, Perseus frisked his way down the lane, clearly happy at the notion of another ride. He did not usually enjoy so many outings when stabled at Havensbeck Manor.

Yet for all his mount's enthusiasm, Matthias could only wish Perseus longer-legged and faster-paced at this moment.

This morning he had opened his eyes to the same curtain-shrouded dimness as every morning in his house. He had lain there in that blank moment, as one did, and then sleepily slid his hand across the sheets in the blank space beside him.

She was not there.

Bernadette was not there.

That thought had sat Matthias upright in his bed with his eyes wide and yes, his jaw actually hanging. All these years he not been able to imagine a life without Marianna. He had clung to her so fiercely.

Yet Marianna had gone ahead, leaving him behind. And now he felt his torn heart whole and strong and pumping again. It stuttered when Bernadette smiled. It swelled when she laughed at him. It pounded like a galloping horse at the thought of waking up next to her.

Bernadette. It was so simple. He must be a fool not to have seen it before. He felt quite brilliant for having seen it at last.

She had read his half-mad ravings and not been repulsed. She had endured his stiff and awkward company and not faltered in her friendship. She had given him the truth, had shown him her flaws and confessed her transgressions, when she might easily have shielded herself.

She was no perfect vision. She was no angelic creation. She was a woman, in turns funny and generous, or outlandish and forthright. A woman real and warm and alive. A woman who had come to him, even knowing what she knew, and had given him back his spirit.

Who was to say that she had not been meant to find those letters? After all, hundreds of people lived downriver from Havensbeck. Why had his heart-broken missives gone to someone who had known terrible loss, and who, however unlikely, was the one person who could show him how to go on again?

Miracles were not a form of belief he'd ever taken stock in. Until now.

Bernadette was his miracle, found by his river, drawn by his need, and now awaiting him a mere half-mile away. In his headlong rush to live again, he spared only a single moment of doubt.

What if she did not feel the same?

She had kissed him. *Well, I kissed her, but she did not draw back.* That was important, was it not?

He was quite sure he had not invented falling in love again. People must've been doing it for all of time. It was only that, on this Christmas morning, opening his eyes had somehow opened them on an entire new, adventurous, vibrant future. His future with Miss Bernadette Goodrich.

Therefore, although the hour might be considered dreadfully early for most of the *ton*, Matthias rang for his valet and began to prepare himself for a ride.

Jasper came to his room. "My lord, you do not have a valet here, remember?"

Matthias turned to Jasper urgently. "I'm going courting. What do I wear? I haven't the vaguest notion how to do this. It's been so long. Do you think she likes blue? It's Christmas day. Ought I to wear the green? Not black. No. No more black."

A strange burbling noise came from the butler. Matthias looked askance at Jasper's face. There was something wrong with it. The usual unflappable mien had cracked in half, broken wide by a smile such as Matthias had never seen on his faithful retainer.

"The green," Jasper said with definitive nod. Then he turned around, still grinning, opened the bedchamber door and stuck his head out into the hallway. "I'll need hot water, boot polish, and something very quick for his lordship's breakfast. Have that hellish beast saddled and brought round the front in a quarter of an hour. Himself is going a-courting!"

Matthias heard the curious sound of several people uttering restrained and muffled cheers. How many of his staff were out there?

Turning, he caught a glimpse of himself in the mirror over his wash-stand. His hair looked strange. He turned to Jasper. "What does my hair look strange?"

Jasper shook his head. "Don't panic, my lord. All will be well."

Matthias turned back to the mirror, plucking a lock of his hair and pulling it forward to stare at with his eyes crossed. "It's so *black*. Has it always been so black?"

Still with a small, irrepressible smile on his face, Jasper rubbed his hands together. "It's high time we began to get you ready, my lord."

Now, Perseus's pounding hoof-beats were as nothing next to the thundering of Matthias's own heart. Every stride of the great long-legged stallion down the lane toward the village brought Matthias closer to the object of his own heart's desire.

Bernadette.

AFTER CRANSTON SHOWED him into a small private parlor at the inn, promising to inform Miss Goodrich of his presence, Matthias waited with barely restrained impatience. He tried to sit, but he couldn't hold still. He found himself pacing and tried to quiet his restless manner. If he didn't gain control of himself, he was going to lunge at Miss Goodrich the moment she walked in the door.

She entered.

Matthias turned toward her eagerly, then forced himself to clasp his hands behind his back. He bobbed a quick bow. "Miss Goodrich. Good morning! Are you well after our adventure last night? I just came to see if you were well. Are you well?"

She remained standing just inside the door. There was an unfamiliar immobility about her. Her hands were still, clasped neatly together before her. Her small smile of greeting looked not a thing like her at all.

Greatly concerned, he took a step forward. "Is Simon all right? I was sure I had him warmly wrapped."

She gave a gracious nod. "Simon is very well, thank you. He slept well and his appetite is not in the least diminished. He is currently partaking of the sweets tray that Mr. Cranston provided us."

"Oh. That's, ah, excellent news." Blast it man, just say it! "Miss Goodrich, I thought perhaps that you might like to learn a bit more about our valley."

She looked at him. "I also live in this valley, my lord. Merely somewhat downriver."

Matthias cleared his throat. "Yes. Yes, you do. But we are very proud of our village. And I think I speak for everyone when I say that your presence, along with that of your aunt and uncle and your brother, has been most enlivening for Haven and Havensbeck Manor."

A small crease formed between her brows. "Enlivening? One hopes that is a good thing. I should not like to think that we have *enlivened* away our welcome."

Matthias writhed inside. He was going about this all wrong. *She'd given him her truth, unvarnished and unexcused.*

He took a steadying breath. "Miss Goodrich, I admire you." *I dream of you.* "I should very much like you to stay longer." He blundered onward. "I wish to know you better. For you to know me.

For us to know each other."

He saw comprehension dawn upon her features. Matthias rushed on. "I mean to say, I should like to call upon you, Miss Goodrich. As a suitor." There, he'd said it. He felt himself grinning like an idiot in sheer relief. He'd actually said it! "I like you, Miss Goodrich. Very much."

It was only then that he noticed the strange look on her face. In fact, she seemed to be suffering from some sort of vertigo. An absent portion of his mind took note of how much he admired the extra ginger dots across the tops of her cheeks that showed better in her pallor.

Her lips were pressed tightly together and her eyes focused unseeing upon his cravat as if she were frozen in fear. Her lips parted but only the strangest little breath of a sound came out. In that moment of hesitation, the door to the little parlor opened and Mrs. Goodrich bustled in.

"Lord Matthias! Heavens, that Cranston fellow didn't tell me it was *you* who called upon us!" The elder vicar's wife stepped forward and beamed sternly at Matthias. Matthias, having never been the recipient of Mrs. Goodrich's smile before, blinked and smiled hesitantly in return.

He bowed. "Mrs. Goodrich, I hope everyone is well this fine Christmas morning?"

From the corner of his eye, Matthias sought thought he saw Bernadette make a slight, fruitless gesture. Then Mrs. Goodrich grabbed his full attention once more.

"Oh, your lordship, it is the grandest of news, is it not? We are all beside ourselves with joy! To think that the children have finally come to their senses and decided to wed! It is all that Vicar Goodrich and I could ever have hoped for!"

The children decided to wed? The children?

Matthias's gaze shot to meet the appalled eyes of Miss Bernadette Goodrich. "Wed." His voice sounded strange in his tight throat. "Are you perhaps referring to Vicar Barton? And?" It could not be. It could not be.

He looked into Bernadette's eyes, or rather, Miss Goodrich's eyes, soon to be the eyes of Mrs. Barton! They were wide and compassionate and yet, also a bit lost. He felt much the same, except he felt enormously lost.

Meanwhile, his tongue took off on its own. "My most sincere congratulations to Vicar Barton! And Miss Goodrich! How very happy I am for you!" If the words came out tortured and strange, Matthias could only wonder that he'd managed to get them out at all.

He bowed awkwardly. Of course, he could not manage to be smooth in such a moment, when he might wish more than ever in his life to be smooth. He bobbed another bow as if to erase the first one, which only became more awkward. His cravat choked him.

Mrs. Goodrich had tilted her silver head and begun to eye him with some reservation. Which one would, when eyeing a man who was swiftly going mad.

"Yes. Yes, best wishes," he blurted. "Best wishes to all. Happy Christmas! Happy, happy, *happy* Christmas."

He bolted from the room before he could be any more ridiculous in his shock and disappointment. Of course, as he fled blindly down the hall, he collided shoulders with Vicar Barton himself. John made a grab for him, as if to steady him. Matthias flinched away.

"My lord? Is all well with you?"

"Happy Christmas." For heaven's sake, stop *saying* that! "Congratulations on your engagement, John." *You are the luckiest foul poaching blackguard who ever lived!*

Jealousy roiled within him. Matthias had no notion how to manage such a forceful and vile sentiment. Yet, what had good John Barton done but see a lovely girl and act without doubt or hesitation upon his proposal?

Leave. Leave now. Leave *faster.*

Matthias left.

He'd been so happy to feel again, after so long existing in the twilight. Now his breath filtered only partly into a chest too tight to inhale.

How he longed for a bit of his former numbness now.

How very painful.

Chapter 16

I N THE INN parlor, Bernadette stood quite still. She was certain she expressed nothing of what she was feeling. And if her fingernails bit slightly too hard into her palms? Well, that was no one's concern but hers.

I like you. Very much.

Oh, how she had made a muck of it all! The man she loved wanted her as well. Wasn't that what every girl dreamed of? It was only too bad she was already engaged to someone else.

She had missed him by an hour. For the rest of her life she would feel the burn of that sore loss.

One hour.

Aunt Sarah was still staring after the departed Lord Matthias. "Well, that is a very strange man. I suppose it comes from being so well-off."

"His wife died in a fire," Bernadette said faintly. "And his little son, too."

"Oh yes. I recall that now." Aunt Sarah did not like being caught being uncharitable. Therefore, she glared at Bernadette with exasperation. "Well, you might have reminded me sooner."

Bernadette looked at her aunt for a long moment. *Perhaps if you were kinder at the outset, you would have fewer regrets later on.* Wise words for all, indeed. "Well, his lordship did not hear you say it."

"Well, the Lord God did!" Aunt Sarah looked down at her hands. "I should not speak unkindly of him. I do not dislike the man. It was only that, well, he was turning your head! And anyone could see he wasn't serious!"

"Oh, he was entirely serious," Bernadette said tonelessly. "He came here this morning to court me, if I allowed it. He told me so."

It was almost worth the pain to see Aunt Sarah's jaw drop in that fashion. "But he's a lord. A peer! What? He couldn't possibly want *you*!"

"As always, my dearest aunt, your faith in me does my heart good." She felt rather tired. Though she'd only woken a few hours past, she felt as though a year had passed since the sun rose.

John Barton entered the parlor. With great relief, Aunt Sarah greeted him. Wisely, Aunt Sarah said nothing of Lord Matthias, even when John asked.

"Where was his lordship going in such tremendous haste? Is he ill? He did not look well."

Bernadette drifted to the window to look out. "Did he not? How curious."

"Well! I think I can leave the two of you alone for a moment. I must check on the vicar. If I don't stop him he'll stuff himself on sweets, and acquire himself a bellyache for his troubles."

Bernadette turned her head and looked her aunt in the eye. "Mind you keep Simon from a similar fate, if you please."

Aunt Sarah blinked at her cold tone, then nodded shortly. "Of course, dear."

As Aunt Sarah fled the room minus some of her usual bustle, John joined Bernadette by the window. "It is Christmas day. Simon was brought home, safe and sound. This morning you agreed to marry me." He turned to face her directly. She kept her gaze averted. "Why are you not happy? Please, look at me, Bernie."

Bernadette.

She lifted her chin and met his gaze. She'd never been able to hide her feelings well. They always seem to come bubbling forth no matter what she did. So she was not surprised when he gazed at her expression with some alarm.

"What is it? My dear, what has happened?"

Perhaps it was selfish of her. Yet in all honesty, Bernadette longed to tell someone who might care. "It seems Lord Matthias came to court me. I believe he intended it in all great seriousness."

Oddly, John did not seem much surprised. Her attention focused quite sharply. She narrowed her eyes. "You knew this. How could you already know this?"

John looked uncomfortable. "It is simply something one man knows about another. When they both care for a lady. There is a certain amount of, well, unspoken competition."

"Competition. Over me?" Then she drew in a quick breath. "Was that why you proposed last night, when I'd only been here a few days? After all those years of not knowing me at all, it did seem a bit of a hurry, but I never dreamed!" She took a step back. "Were you simply trying to *win*?"

John looked quite properly horrified at the notion. That was reassuring in one way and also not. "I should say not! It was my very intention when I invited your family all to join me here. I told you last night, I have been waiting to be in a position to support a wife properly. I've been planning for years. First my education, then a good position, then a wife. I mean, then you."

If she was not a prize, was she, perhaps, merely part of a plan? *Am I your Marianna, or not?* "Last night, why did you propose?" She shook her head. "I suppose it doesn't matter now. We are engaged. The matter is finished."

She let her gaze drift to the window once more. "I imagine we will have a few uncomfortable moments dealing with his lordship in the future. Still, he is an honorable man and not unkind. I'm sure he will behave quite properly."

She thought about his abrupt and bizarre departure. *That is, once he no longer mourns my loss.* She dare not forget that Lord Matthias felt things most deeply. He was not a man to get over his feelings easily. Oh, she had struck him such a terrible blow when he was so close to healing at last.

Another thing I shall regret forever.

"And what of you, Bernadette?"

It was the first time John had ever called her by her full name. She lifted her head and gazed at him sharply. "What you mean?"

John gazed at her for a long moment and then let out a breath. "I'm looking at you now and it's as if you are not standing before me. You have gone away somewhere. I'm not sure how but it seems as though I am at fault." He reached out a hand as if to brush back a strand of hair from her face. Heaven help her, she shifted away. A look of resignation closed John's usually open expression.

"You love him."

She wouldn't lie, not to this good man. Not to herself. "I do love him. And I have for many years."

At John's very evident surprise at that fact, Bernadette explained the messages in the bottles, the years of waiting for them to arrive every Christmas, the poring over them for hours by candlelight.

"So you see, my good, kind, generous John, I have been guilty from the start. I do not deserve you. Nor him. I am, as Aunt Sarah would say, an irredeemable wretch."

John abruptly turned away from her and crossed the room with his head down and his hands clasped firmly behind his back. He stood before the fire but she did not think he saw the blue flames dancing on the coals. "So why did you agree to marry me?" His deep voice was very quiet.

"For my family, of course." She did not intend to be harsh, merely to continue her new habit of honesty.

A long breath. "Well, of course you would not do such a thing for yourself. Very understandable." He nodded and took a deep breath. "That's all there is then." He turned sharply to face her.

"My dear Miss Goodrich, I do release you from our agreement of one hour. I rather think I should like to wed someone who truly wishes to wed me. Suddenly that seems highly important. Highly important indeed."

Bernadette stared at him. Released? How strange. She thought she stood wrapped around in chains, that her future was as fixed as a stone buried so deep into the earth that it looked like a mere pebble until one tried to dig it up! A few words of truth from her lips and she was released?

Take it, foolish girl, take it and run! "I thank you most kindly, Vicar Barton." She gave a curtsy, for something seemed called for. "You are absolutely deserving to be truly loved. I'm sure you shall be, very soon."

She was suddenly seized by restless energy. Freed from her polite cage her hands fluttered up almost of their own will. She went up on tiptoe and settled back down. She moved one step to the side, turned to the window, turned back to John and shook her head. "I don't know what to do with myself."

John gazed at her ruefully. Frown creased his brow as he watched her strange restless dance. "You are an impatient thing. Are you going to see him now?"

"Yes." *Oh, yes-yes-yes!*

He tilted his head. "And suddenly you are even more attractive than you were ten minutes ago. Love suits you."

Bernadette blushed and turned to leave. Just as she had her hand on the latch of the door, she turned half-around again.

"I don't think I was your Marianna, after all."

John looked at her sadly, not questioning what she intended by that. "I think you could have been. I really do."

MATTHIAS DISMOUNTED PERSEUS at his own front steps and left the great snorting beast to the groom. It was rare that Matthias allowed his mount to gallop uncontrolled for so long. Perseus had mightily enjoyed the race back to Havensbeck.

Matthias had simply wanted to get as far away from the future vicar and Mrs. Barton as he could. Oh damn, she would be the wife of the vicar of his own village. Oh, no.

He should depart for London immediately. Yes, at once. Of course, he hated London, too. But at least there he would not be seeing those eyes laughing at someone else, that smile directed at another man, and if his hearth and bed were condemned to be cold and empty forever, at least he could be as far from the source of his pain as possible.

The first time he had felt his heart warm from its long winter, and he'd been too scared, too slow, too lost in the woods to see clearly in time.

He had loved once. Somehow, he had managed to find his way to love again. He most sincerely doubted his heart would ever recover enough for a third assault.

Jasper met him at the door and took his hat and coat eagerly. "How was your ride, my lord? You are back rather quickly. Will you be returning to Haven again today? Is it something you'll be doing often?

"Jasper, blast it, leave off! She's marrying the vicar!" There. That should put a stop to Jasper's matchmaking. "I'm going to my study." He wouldn't scandalize Jasper by asking for brandy at this early hour. Besides, he was fairly certain he had a bottle left in his desk.

He didn't desire to drink, in the end. He stood in his study and gazed out at the soft gray winter's day, the fresh snow as tender as a dove's wing. Last night's weather was a kindly sort of snowfall, merely enough to beautify the trampled, dirtied white, as if to say,

"Happy Christmas to all."

I do believe this puts paid to me ever enjoying Christmas again. Yes, I am quite sure of it.

Jasper brought coffee, steaming bitter and aromatic in the silver server. Wise Jasper.

Once he'd served, Jasper stayed, poising himself in the center of the carpet with his hands behind his back, like a penitent tradesman or guilty tenant. Matthias frowned at him. "What is it, Jasper?"

"My lord, it was all my fault."

Matthias closed his eyes, too weary even for exasperation. "What is all your fault, Jasper?"

The butler lifted his chin, as if preparing for a blow. "It was I who went to Vicar Barton and asked him to invite Vicar Goodrich's family for Christmas."

That fixed Matthias's attention. He scowled at Jasper. "You did *what*?"

"My lord, it was the letter. Do you remember the letter, from the girl who laughed so hard she sat on the sundial?"

Matthias bristled. "That letter could not have possibly come from Bernadette Goodrich! The woman who wrote it was barely literate!"

"I do believe, upon further reflection, my lord, that the letter was from young master Simon. I suspect he was doing a bit of matchmaking for his sister."

Matthias shook his head. "Perhaps he was, but at what point did you decide that the semi-literate letter writer ought to come here to be my bride?"

Jasper swallowed at Matthias's tone, but forged on bravely. "It was the laughter, my lord. It has been so many years since this house has known laughter. We, the staff and I, well, we want it back."

Matthias passed both hands over his face, trying to scrub away the sticky spider web of Jasper's intricate logic. "So, in order to find me an illiterate bride, you go to the village vicar and ask him to please invite his long-lost love to Haven so she can dance with me at a ball?"

Jasper squirmed. "Well, not *intentionally,* my lord."

Matthias couldn't help it. It was the strangest thing. He was desperately unhappy. His heart was broken anew. Yet from somewhere deep inside him, helpless laughter began to fizz. He leaned his rear on the edge of his desk for a moment with his hands over his face and simply shook.

"My lord?"

"Oh Sweet Christmas Bells on a Stick!" Matthias dropped his hands to grip the sides of the desk and begin to laugh. The sounds he uttered were rusty and long unused, like hinges on a door too long shut. He laughed. He roared.

Jasper, wisely, waited it out without further comment.

Finally, Matthias drew a long, shuddering breath and wiped his eyes. Those were tears of laughter. He would admit to no other sort at this moment. "Jasper? Would you kindly fetch fresh paper and ink? And an empty bottle, please. I have one last letter to write."

WHEN BERNIE CAME in sight of the carriage bridge across the river, she saw a lone figure standing at the wall, gazing down at the water. Her heart fluttered within her ribs like a captive bird sensing freedom. Her steps quickened.

When she came abreast of Lord Matthias, she saw an empty wine bottle standing on the wall beside its cork. In his hands he held a single sheet of paper.

"Am I disturbing you? It seems a private moment."

He must not have heard her steps over the rushing of the river for he turned quickly, startled. His elbow struck the bottle, knocking it from its perch on the wall.

Both Bernadette and Matthias leaned over the wall to watch it fall. When it disappeared into the churning water running between the jagged ice banks, she turned to him with a frown. "Shall I fetch you another? I shouldn't mind it all. It was my fault."

"Now. No, that's quite alright." He straightened to face her.

She remembered something and held up one hand to halt him as she dug in her pocket. When she drew out a large stack of parchment, folded carefully and tied with a green hair ribbon and presented it to him, he stared at it without comprehension.

She pushed the gift closer. "These are yours. I am returning them to you."

"Oh." He blinked at that. "Yes." He took them from her gingerly, taking care their hands did not touch. "Well, I suppose it would be rather inappropriate for my village vicar's wife to have them."

She noticed with a bittersweet amusement that he could barely meet her eyes. *It may take me a lifetime to make that up to him.*

That sounded just fine to her.

"Matthias," her tone was gentle. "I had thought to tease you with this, but I fear I'm no good at keeping secrets anymore. John Barton has released me from our agreement."

Matthias's eyes widened slightly and he swayed toward her as if pulled by gravity itself. "What does that mean, released you? How? He has ended your engagement?" Conflicting emotions ran across his face. Bernadette wondered how anyone could ever think him distant or unreadable.

He looked as though he couldn't decide whether he ought to find John Barton and hug him or challenge him to a duel for Bernadette's honor. She found she quite liked that quality in a man.

Her joy begin to effervescence within her. She cast him the brightest smile she had and watched him blink against the glow. "Matthias, I am quite eligible now. And I believe there was something you were going to say to me?"

"I do. I have something I very much want to say to you. But there's something I have to do first." He held out the single folded sheet in his hand. "One last letter."

She looked at the paper for a long moment. "I see. Well then, I should leave you to it."

He held out a hand, though he stopped short of quite touching her arm. "I'd like you to stay, if you would. It is a goodbye letter."

Bernadette felt her heart lighten further. "I should be honored to remain, if that is what you wish."

She could not take her eyes off the missive in his hand. A smile tugged at the corners of his mouth, lending a sweet and boyish quality to his usually stern features. "Would you like to read it?"

Bernadette put her hands behind her back and clasped them virtuously together. "No, indeed. This has nothing to do with me. It's a private matter."

He tilted his head and his smile grew, but just on one side, as if he was slightly out of practice. Her heart melted.

"You really want to read it, don't you?"

She chewed her lip for a moment. "Well, yes. Yes, I would very much like to read it, thank you."

He handed the letter to her and she carefully unfolded it.

My dearest Marianna and my darling Simon,

Wherever you are, you need not wait for me any longer. I have decided to stay right where I am. I will smile, and laugh, and makes snow doggies, and hang green things in the manor at Christmastime. I will do all of these things for you who cannot, and for myself because it seems I quite like them.

I am awake now. Let your sleep be easy. I am going to be fine.

My everlasting love to you both,

M

Bernadette felt her breath come shakily as she tenderly refolded the note and placed it back in Matthias's hand. He closed his fingers over it and tucked it into the stack of earlier letters. He looked at them for a long moment. Then he tugged the ribbon free and let all the letters fall.

They fluttered like doves, swirling down through the air until they were caught and carried away by the rushing water. The river took them, and this time the river would not give them up so easily.

Bernadette stepped closer to him and leaned her cheek against his shoulder. "Did you know that I would be coming back to you today?"

"No. I thought you quite gone from me. I believed myself alone in the world."

"It makes me very happy to know that you were ready to live on, whether or not you knew you were to live on with me." She pulled the glove from her hand and lifted her fingers to touch his dear face. "If I were her, I would be very content right now."

"I think that I am very glad that you are nothing like Marianna. You are everything that is Bernadette, instead. Tremendous, sometimes a bit frightening, possibly devastating. That is perfectly wonderful, as far as I'm concerned. That is my Bernadette."

She smiled at him again. He reached for her bare hand and wrapped it in both his large ones. He pressed her palm his chest. "I am setting the past free. The pain of the past and the love of the past. I wish to make room in my home, in my world, and in my heart."

Bernadette tilted her head and gave him a joyous chortle. "I think that's an excellent notion! Because you do realize that I come with a little brother? And I daresay I'd like to keep my aunt and uncle quite close to hand."

He smiled and stepped a little closer. "It is a very large manor. I believe there is room for all the Goodriches and perhaps a few more Waterfords as well."

She matched his approach, coming closer step for step. Gazing up into his deep blue eyes, she sighed. "Is that a proposal, my lord?"

"No, Miss Bernadette Goodrich, it is a vow. I have released my last letter. I have released the past. You, my love, I am keeping. You are my Christmas gift and it is very bad form to return a gift!"

He lowered his mouth to hers in a sweet, chaste kiss. *Devastating, am I?* Bernadette dared to part her lips. In answer to her boldness, he slid one big hand into her hair and cupped her skull in his palm as the kiss deepened.

She forgot the snow and the cold in the heat of his mouth. The lost soul was found again and his restored strength bolstered her even as it seduced her. By the time they parted, they were both breathless and smiling loopy grins at each other.

"Let us go home," he said. He took her hand and they crossed the river, left the bridge behind, and walked together up to the holly-infested manor house. "Shall we set the wedding date for the feast of St. Valentine?"

After that kiss? Not likely! Bernie raised a brow. "I think perhaps I'd prefer the eve of the New Year!"

At his rusty bark of laughter, Bernadette leaned her head on his arm and sighed with the depth of her contentment. "Happy Christmas, my Lord Matthias."

"Happy Christmas, my mad Miss Goodrich."

Read on for the introductory chapters of the
second **Haven Holiday** story by Celeste Bradley!

While You Were Dreaming

*Haven's vicar John Barton still carries a torch for Bernadette, now the
happily married lady of Havensbeck Manor. When a carriage accident
quite literally drops the unconscious beauty, Lady Emmeline Grey, into
his arms, John begins to think perhaps he might just be able to leave his
hopeless love behind him. If only Lady Emmeline's irritating cousin,
Norah Grey, would stay out of his way!*

While You Were Dreaming

Chapter 1

V ICAR JOHN BARTON took the last nail into his hand and hefted his hammer once more. Pounding the finishing nail into the last framing board around the final window of the entire house should have been a triumph. The large but drafty old vicarage had been reborn into a spacious, snug home bright with fresh paper on the walls and fine glass windows. He'd begun the work when he'd first arrived in Haven a little over two years past. Only the painting of the last few window frames remained.

John should have been exultant. Instead he only felt edgy and cold.

It was not the proper season for building. It was December, lacking only a few days until Christmas. And December in Staffordshire was no summer day in Brighton!

Yet John had been determined to finish his vicarage. Furthermore, he needed to keep busy so as not to dwell upon the lord of Havensbeck and his lady, getting ready to put on their first Christmas celebration as a wedded couple at the manor. All of Haven was invited. John's invitation had been penned by her ladyship herself, the warm greeting simple, the wistful request an act of reconciliation toward a family friend.

He would never receive any other sort of message from her now. That ship had sailed, that stable door had been left open, that water had turned to ice under the bridge—and Matthias was a bloody, greedy poaching bastard!

Except he wasn't. Lord Matthias was a good man and a dedicated, responsible landlord who took excellent care of Haven and all its residents. In fact, he and John had almost become friends before John had encouraged pretty Bernie and her family to spend the previous Christmas in Haven.

John had thought himself clever, timing it all so well. He would spend some time with Bernadette, whom he'd begun to care for a very long time ago but who'd never much noticed him, all the while with the enthusiastic support of his former mentor, Bernadette's uncle, who favored the match. John would show Bernadette his very fine vicarage and the lovely village and when he'd beguiled her with his success, he would propose.

And he had.

And she'd accepted him. It had all been storybook perfect— except that even before he'd had the opportunity to make an impression on the new, adult Bernadette, she'd already unhorsed Lord Matthias into a snowdrift and irrevocably captured his lordship's attention. A momentary encounter on a country road had overturned every single meticulously planned detail of John's courtship.

John hammered more violently for a moment, picturing a certain poaching rake of a lord sitting upon the head of his nail. Then the anger subsided, as it always did, because Matthias wasn't a rake or a poacher. He'd been a man lost in mourning for the wife and child he'd lost tragically several years before. Since he'd come to Haven, John had racked his brain for some way to help Matthias.

Well, John had certainly helped him, by bringing the one person who carried within her a certain spark, a clear, brilliant vitality that shone from her lovely eyes—and yes, with enough experience with her own tragedy to help a broken man move on from his. Bernie had even brought along a new child, her worldly-wise little brother Simon, to brighten the dark halls of Havensbeck.

At the thought of Simon, John put the hammer down and drank a swig of tepid, overly steeped tea. He grimaced at the taste. He couldn't seem to make a decent pot of tea for himself. He ought to go inside and warm himself at the hearth, but the sun was still on the crystalline valley and the days were so short now. He couldn't bear to spend a moment of it indoors.

Young Simon would be climbing the walls on a day like today, wanting to be outside. John felt the same way, edgy and twitching with house-bound restiveness. The sun was bright on the snow and the wind was slight, giving the day a deceptively balmy feel. John had lived in Haven long enough to know better. The ice was thick on the River Churnet and the night would fall black and impenetrable in just a few hours.

John stepped back and looked at his handiwork.

Building things wasn't what he'd been raised to do. His father would likely shudder at the very idea, yet John had found real enjoyment in the use of his healthy body and his new, hard-won skills.

Now, the exterior window frames were entirely complete. Every window had fine new glass and a spacious windowsill. He'd designed deep sills for the single shining memory of young Bernadette curled up on a sunny windowsill of her uncle's vicarage, lost in a book. The sun had glinted on her amber-brown hair and the light had shone into her eyes, making her squint resentfully though she was clearly too enraptured by what she was reading to bother adjusting her position. She'd been no more than a gawky fifteen and he'd been just another boring adult, albeit a young one. She'd been polite to him when she remembered he existed, but she'd never invited him into that personal, clearly magical world behind those eyes.

John had been an awkward and officious twenty, very aware of his own importance as the selected student of the venerated Vicar Goodrich. Young Bernie mocked him politely for his determination to bring God to the world whether the world liked it or not, and Vicar Goodrich had shown him a gentler approach of guidance and support. Vicar Goodrich had led John by example, bestowing grace in constant small doses that brought succor and strength to everyone around him. A new ambition had been born in John, to set aside the fire and brimstone he'd been taught to favor, and instead to serve with generosity and patience.

And to do it with Bernadette Goodrich at his side.

He'd been so relieved when his scrawny, spotty youthful looks had improved and it became likely that a young lady would not be averse to becoming the vicar's wife. John's only hope was that clever, lively Bernie might feel the same.

So close. He'd missed making that impression upon her by a bloody hour!

John sighed and closed his eyes. *You are the vicar.* "I shall not curse." He looked skyward. "Sorry."

The empty house didn't comment. The spacious rooms and the

fine new windowsills and the impervious roof simply sat there, offering nothing in return for his hard work.

The feeling gripped him again, that need for action, for desperate occupation so that he could fall exhausted into his cold bed at night and not spend hours imagining the Christmas he might have been having this year with his beloved new family.

One bloody hour.

He ran his hand through his saw-dusted hair and squinted at the bright day once more. He had close to three hours before night fell.

STUPID. BLOODY. ROCK!

John didn't even bother to pronounce his anti-cursing ritual. He was one chunk of sandstone short of a full load in his mule-cart and the small white sun hung so low on the hillside across the river that it looked as if it might roll right down the snowy slope. It was already growing dark in the cut of the river.

He should leave now, if he wished to get the cart home before full dark. He would just have to come back another time for the last stone. It wasn't as if he would even be able to lay the stone on the terrace until spring. Sometimes he doubted his own good sense. Yes, he should definitely go.

Instead he dug his pry bar into the crack between the frozen ground and the large hunk of sandstone he had ambitiously chosen. This was meant to be a cost-saving measure, not a penance. It didn't hurt that it was one less thing he would have to request from his lordship. Matthias would shrug and order the finest flagstones the quarries downriver could cut. Then every time John walked upon them, he would recall that his life and his work was entirely dependent upon the support of the man who had stolen the woman John had set his heart on.

Grunting, John pounded the pry bar deeper with a few strikes of his sledgehammer, then he put all his weight into shifting the rock. The exertion made his cold, tired body ache and his head pound.

For just a bit more strength, he cast his thoughts back to the sight of Bernadette and Matthias, with their coats covering their wedding garb, leaving the Havensbeck chapel to be greeted by every single denizen of Haven, all equally bundled up, who had cast cut paper snowflakes at the sheepishly grinning couple in lieu of flower petals. Bernie, laughing, alight with joy. Matthias, gobsmacked by his own good fortune and most definitely smug about it.

Weeks. Mere weeks of courtship. Bernie had been so mad for Matthias, and he for her, that John had taken the high road and stepped aside—and Matthias hadn't lost a moment in making his conquest.

"*Rraahh!*" Spurred by the twist of the knife of memory, John convulsed his entire body, aiming all his disappointment and fury and hurt at the pry bar—and ripped the wide, flat piece of sandstone from the frozen earth.

As if in answer, a high, feminine scream cut the icy air.

JOHN FOLLOWED THE cry, running along the riverbank, slipping in the snow. Ahead he could see the silhouette of the bridge against the dimming sky and the shadow play of a damaged carriage tilting slowly, slowly over the stone balustrade of the bridge.

The neighing of distressed horses echoed the screams. He kept running, scrambling up the bank now to access the bridge level.

"Hold on!"

More cries from the carriage. "Help! I can't hold her. She's falling!"

John looked up to see a limp form hanging from the carriage that still threatened to topple over the edge of the bridge. Then he realized why. One of the horses had already fallen over the side and was now dangling from its harness, screaming in panic and thrashing wildly. Every convulsion of its giant body tore at the carriage, dragging it down, crushing it against the low stone wall, while the other panicked horse, still on the bridge but fighting the pull with all its might, threatened to rip the vehicle apart with its plunging antics.

The lady in the silk gown hung pale and unmoving except for the limp sway of her upper body as she hung with her lower half and skirt trapped within the carriage.

It only took a split of a second for John to assess the situation and make a decision. He'd never be able to secure the carriage in time, for the dangling horse was doing more damage by the moment. "I'm getting below her! I'll catch her!"

"Hurry!"

John scrambled down the rocky bank and slithered awkwardly out onto the ice until he stood just beneath the insensible lady. She'd slipped a bit farther out of the carriage. The other woman must be losing her grip.

"Now! Let her go!" John cried over the wheezing and groaning of the trapped horse, whose rear hooves whipped the air in alarming nearness to John's upraised arms.

The lady fell silently, with only the flutter of her skirts and cape to mark her descent. As she turned in the air, John had a brief impression of black and white and scarlet before she landed in his arms and knocked him back hard onto the ice. The wind left his lungs in a great whoosh and his arse ached, only partially protected by his thick woolen coat, but he'd caught her!

As he tried to bring any possible scrap of air back into his chest, he looked back up at the carriage to spy wide, worried eyes in a pale face, peering down at him and his catch.

"Get free!" he tried to say. Before he could gather the breath to shout a warning, the harness broke into pieces, the sounds like gunshots as the leather straps rent and the traces snapped—

And the horse fell.

Chapter 2

J OHN WRAPPED HIS arms about the lady and rolled. As he'd feared, the massive crack of the ice behind him marked the horse's impact. He kept rolling, for there was no time to stand and lift and run—

He felt the crack run beneath him, cutting through the ice near his ribcage. The world shifted and rolled and John knew that the ice was shattering beneath them. He scrambled to his knees and grabbed a fistful of silk, crawling desperately toward the bank before the ice broke into floes too small to hold them and they slipped into the deathly river. He might survive it—it was not his first encounter with failing ice—but the injured woman in his arms would sink like a stone, her skirts so heavy with water that she'd not be able to remain above the ice even if she were fully conscious and a strong swimmer.

He grabbed at the ice where it had frozen into raised rivulets and pushed hard with his boots and pulled his charge with all his might. He practically threw her up onto the bank as his trailing feet sank beneath the water and all sensation in his legs ended.

"Emmeline! Em! Oh, wake up Em! Wake up!"

John blinked vaguely up at the person on the bank now kneeling over the unconscious lady. "A hand, madam," he wheezed, "if you do not mind?"

The person crawled toward him, grabbed two fistfuls of his coat and leaned back from the river. This was surprisingly helpful, enabling John to drag himself free of the deadly cold water tugging forcefully at his feet. Clearly the lady was a sturdy sort.

They both turned at a great splashing and snorting to see the fallen carriage horse clambering ashore not far from them. John stared in astonishment, for he'd assumed the beast was doomed by its fall.

Next to him, a voice snarled. "Of course, the idiot creature survived, it being all his fault! Poor Emmeline!"

John turned to examine his helper for the first time. She was very pale, with ruddy blotches of worry and distress upon her cheeks as she gazed down at her unconscious companion. Round-faced and freckled with pale brows and lashes, the worried lady wore a gray woolen cloak over a dark-colored dress.

John looked down at the woman he still held close and the breath left his body at her still pale beauty. The white he'd seen was the ivory of her perfect complexion. The black was her shining hair tumbling over the snow. The startling red was the blood that traced rivulets over her brow and cheek. She was clad in purple silk and her matching cloak was lined in fur.

His pounding heart skipped a beat. She looked like misplaced royalty. As if she'd heard that stuttering pulse, the woman stirred slightly and opened eyes of such a rich and stunning blue that John's mind could only come up with the word "violet".

She blinked up at him, her gaze unfocused and vague. "My...angel," she whispered before her lids fell shut once more.

She was the most beautiful woman John had ever seen.

"You'll both die of chill shortly, so kindly stop mooning over Lady Emmeline before you're so cold that you'll be of no use whatsoever!"

The annoyed tone shook John free from his gobsmacked state. The sharp-tongued woman was entirely correct. He had already lost sensation in his wet feet and the injured lady needed to be seen to immediately.

However, John was not accustomed to being spoken to as if he were nothing more than a foolish servant. Deciding that any reply he might make now would only be something to regret later, he held back his retort and clambered awkwardly to his numb feet.

Getting the unconscious beauty up the slick, snow-covered bank required cooperation, which brought about more caustic commentary from the gray-cloaked woman. Repressing his irritation in favor of saving lives, as any gentleman would do, John followed the woman's snarled orders until they reach the high point of the bank and were able to follow the snowy lane. The woman then ran ahead to where the carriage still canted dangerously over the low stone wall of the bridge.

"Mr. Higgins? Mr. Higgins!" The woman flung herself forward, skidding to her knees on the packed, trampled snow and crawling beneath the carriage.

Foolish female! With his arms full of his own rescue, John could do little to stop the lady's companion from endangering herself. Then he saw that she scooted backward out of the space beneath the spinning wheels with her fists full of someone's burly arm. The missing driver!

She glared at John over her shoulder as she tugged. "Oh for pity's sake! Just go lead the horse onward for a few yards, so I can get to Mr. Higgins properly!"

John moved to do just that. The second horse, still mostly in its harness, was somewhat the worse for wear than its companion who now clopped wearily along the bridge toward them, having followed John. The still-harnessed horse stood bracing its own weight against the pull of the tilting carriage, its hide covered in sweat, with foam forming around its bit. The creature was clearly in great distress.

With his arm full of woman, John could just about free one hand to grab the trailing rein. "Come along, lad. Shh. All is well. Quiet."

The horse rolled him a disbelieving eye, but responded with a small reluctant step when John let him onward. The carriage shuddered. Another step, and another. The carriage teetered.

"Beware!" John called back over his shoulder, his voice muffled by the folds of the lady's cloak piled against his neck. He ought to put her down, but where? She was so cold already it hardly seemed a good notion to lie her down on the snow.

"Come along," he urged the horse. "Just a step, lad. Just another step."

The carriage creaked mightily, then noisily scraped forward, one side still angled out over the wall. Another step and another, until John heard the gray-cloaked woman cry out.

"We are clear!"

Which was a good thing, for the carriage suddenly fell back upon its four wheels with a crash. The impact collapsed it like a house of cards, turning it to naught but a pile of lacquered firewood.

Oh damn. John released the horse and staggered back to check on the lady's companion and the driver.

Rounding the wreckage, he was stunned to see the woman crouching over the injured man, clearly shielding his body from the debris still falling from the tilted top of the carriage. John gasped to see a large wooden trunk begin to slide directly toward the two on the snowy ground.

There was no time to put the lady down, even had there been a place to put her. With his hands full, all John could do was to thrust his body into the path of the sliding trunk and take the impact on his back and shoulders.

Ouch.

Such a day he'd had.

Deflected by mere flesh and bone, the trunk slithered safely away to fall a few feet past the driver and the lady's companion. Grudging admiration filled him. Annoying as the woman might be, John had to admit she took little care for herself when someone else was in need.

More things rained down upon John's back, baskets and bundles and lightweight hat boxes. He took the small bumps without complaint, but when something burst open and showered him with dainty underthings, John's long-suffering silence shattered.

"Bloody damned *hell!*" He bellowed. He shook his head violently to dislodge something lacy and smelling of lavender water. It only fell down to encircle his neck like a clerical collar.

The driver and the lady's companion were staring up at him in openmouthed shock. Well, that was regrettable. He shook his head. *So sorry.*

John heard voices and looked to see damned Matthias and—oh, but of course!—Bernadette running up the lane to their aid. The manor was just up the rise. Someone must have heard the ruckus.

John resigned himself to helplessly standing there with an unconscious woman in his arms and a set of lacy drawers around his neck.

A snicker erupted at his side. He cast a glance of loathing at the lady's companion. Rude creature, after all he'd done.

It didn't help that once the two injured people had been sorted into the hands of his lordship's excellent staff, Bernie had looked at John with a twist to her lips that told him she repressed a snicker of her own.

With the entire staff rushing to aid them, John was forced to give up his lovely burden. John would have liked to stride into Havensbeck Manor still carrying his rescued lady, making quite the heroic picture. However, there was no denying that during the evening's adventure he'd done something rather awful to his back muscles. He staggered into the great house like a bent old man, bracing himself on door jambs and furniture until he could collapse onto a sofa. It was all he could do not to whimper out loud.

The house's greater concern was for the lady and the driver. Lady Emmeline had a head injury and was unconscious. Mr. Higgins, who had been trapped between the stone side wall of the bridge and the carriage, had suffered a dislocated shoulder and several cracked ribs.

All this John found out when the physician had finished with the injured two and someone—probably Bernie, since John was fairly certain that Matthias thought of him as little as possible—sent the man in John's direction.

"You've pulled a few muscles in your back, lad. Got off lightly, you did. Best to go on home and rest yourself."

Since he could manufacture no excuse to stay, John rubbed his stiffening back and prepared to leave Havensbeck for his vicarage. He would have liked to check in on Lady Emmeline with the otherworldly violet eyes. He even thought to search out the horses, the silly falling one and the brave stalwart one, but it grew very late and it was a long cold walk home.

At the unattended front door, John stopped short. What of his mule? Was the poor thing still standing on the riverbank harnessed to the cart full of stones?

"John?"

Bernadette. John steeled himself to turn toward the woman he'd waited six years to marry.

She looked every inch the lady of the manor she floated toward him with a swish of expensive skirts. She smiled up at him. "You're not leaving now. It's half-past ten and you're exhausted. You're staying here tonight."

It was not a request, or even a demand. Bernie declared it a fact and John, as ever, could refuse her nothing.

"But my mule—"

"Is in the stable, enjoying a hot mash along with Lady Emmeline's carriage horses." She smiled up at him warmly. "All is well and collected, even Lady Emmeline's baggage." Her lips twitched and John knew he was never going to hear the end of Lady Emmeline's lacy drawers. John could only smile back hesitantly. *Oh, Bernie.*

"I must ask you, John," came the deep voice of Lord Matthias from the shadows of the foyer, "whatever were you doing digging stones in the middle of winter?"

John very carefully did not draw back guiltily from Bernadette, for they were doing nothing more than having a conversation. Alone. In the darkened foyer. Bernadette was only being a good hostess, and a good friend. They were not standing particularly close. The moment of intimacy was entirely of John's own imagining.

Or perhaps not, by the steely glint in Matthias's eyes as the lord of the manor stepped into the candlelight.

You've won, John glared back. *Let it go.*

Matthias's gaze narrowed. *I will when you do.*

Bernadette clapped her hands sharply. When both men turned startled expressions upon her, she scowled at them. "If you're finished with your masculine posturing, my love, will you see to our guest? Since you seem somehow dissatisfied with my own actions?" She tilted her head at her glowering husband and smiled so sweetly that John, knowing Bernie well, rather feared for the poaching bastard.

Not a poacher. Not a bastard.

Bernie had a right to choose anyone she liked, and Bernie had chosen Matthias.

Let her go. Think of something else, for pity sake!

The acerbic tone in his own mind made John think of the lady's companion. He didn't know her name. "Ah, what is Lady Emmeline's condition? "

Bernie's expression saddened. "She is still unconscious, poor girl. It seems she struck her head on the stone wall as she was flung out the carriage door. If it had not been for Miss Grey's quick thinking, she'd surely have fallen to her death on the ice!"

Miss Grey had saved the day, had she? All by herself?

THAT BUMBLING DOLT!

Miss Norah Grey gently bathed Emmeline's forehead with a dampened cloth. Em didn't have a fever, but her poor head had taken such a knock that Norah felt it couldn't do any harm.

That idiot, flinging himself—and Emmeline!—into the path of that falling trunk! Norah flinched again, recalling how the solid wood had narrowly missed Emmeline's skull as it glanced off the stupid fellow's thick shoulder.

She knew her anger was irrational, but anger at a stranger seemed a safer direction for her thoughts than remembering the accident. Her memory skidded away from those appalling moments even then. It was easier to blame the man on the bridge than to acknowledge her own failure.

A faint tap at the bedchamber door preceded their hostess, Lady Bernadette, who entered with fresh candles and an efficiently bustling maid.

"I thought you might like to catch a bit of rest, Miss Grey. Higgins will be happy to care for Lady Emmeline for a while."

"No, I—" Norah looked at the maid curiously. "Higgins? Like our driver?"

"My brother, miss," the pretty maid answered. "His lordship himself hired him up from London. Factory work had done my brother ill and I asked milady if we couldn't find something a bit more healthy for him up here in Staffordshire."

Norah blinked. "Healthy? Oh dear."

Lady Bernadette grinned, her smile wide and mischievous. "Oh, don't fret. The physician said he'll be fine in a month, though he'll have a weather-ache in that shoulder. Right now he has half the maids in the house vying to rub a bit of liniment on his... ah... heroic vainglory."

"That's thanks to you, miss," Miss Higgins added with a curtsy. "And he's right besotted now, for it. Miss Grey this and Miss Grey that!" Miss Higgins sent a saucy wink at Norah, who bit her lip in amusement.

"I see. Well, I must give... oh, what is the name of the gentleman who assisted us?"

"The vicar? Oh, that would be John Barton."

The vicar? Really? Norah hoped that God wielded a powerful bar of soap for cursing vicars. "Well, the... the vicar did his part. He caught Emmeline in his arms when she fell from the bridge height—"

"He what?" Lady Bernadette stared at Norah. "Christmas bells!"

Norah decided she liked Lady Bernadette a great deal. Quite frankly, she hadn't expected to do so. When she'd learned of Lord Matthias's invitation for Christmas, she'd worried that the new wife might not appreciate the reminders of the old wife.

Six months past, Lord Matthias's man of business had simply walked up the stairs at Kewell Abbey and stoutly declared that after years of searching the branches of the family tree of Lady Marianna of Havensbeck Manor, the heiress had been found at last. Lady Emmeline Grey, poor daughter of a destitute baron, had received a lavish fortune and a standing invitation to visit Havensbeck Manor at her leisure.

Yet Lord Matthias had remarried. Having the family of your new husband's beloved first wife arrive for an extended visit in the middle of winter? It sounded a bit of a cautionary tale!

Now she could see that Lady Bernadette was only warmly concerned for "Cousin Emmeline".

Norah shrugged. "Well, when the harness broke and the horse fell nearly on top of them and the vicar managed to roll Emmeline out of the ice and onto firm ground—"

Both maid and milady now stared at Norah, agog.

Norah frowned. "Why? What did the vicar say happened?"

Lady Bernadette shook her head slightly. "He said you were very brave and saved both Cousin Emmeline and poor Higgins."

It was Norah's turn to go wide-eyed. "But I didn't! Well, I suppose I—but Emmeline might be dead if not for him."

Lady Bernadette sat back with her arms folded and a cross wrinkle between her brows. "Hang you, John Barton!"

Miss Higgins dusted her hands together. "Now, miss. Let's get you into a nightdress and into bed. You had a ragged sorta day, I'll wager."

Norah opened her mouth to protest that she'd rather stay with Emmeline, but her weary thoughts were no match for Miss Higgins in a zealous bout of efficiency. She found herself tucked in, having been benevolently forced into a quick wash, a hair brushing and braiding, a very luxurious winter nightdress and a wide soft bed in the chamber down the hall from Emmeline's.

Having submitted thus far, she hadn't the mustard to resist the weight of her own drooping eyelids. With only a moment of imagining the tall, brawny vicar snatching Emmeline out of thin air, Norah fell asleep as if she'd been bespelled.

JOHN, HAVING HAD his concerns addressed and knowing that pacing the floor all night over Lady Emmeline's condition wouldn't do a thing to alleviate her danger, forced himself to have a quick wash, accept and don a very luxurious nightshirt—probably belonging to Matthias for it was a good match in size—and lay down upon a bed too wide and soft by far.

Tomorrow he'd have a word with the conniving lady's companion about her tendency to aggrandize herself. Not in a competitive manner, no. More that it was his duty to redirect the path of the selfish onto a way more honorable.

Her mistress, now—there was the very face of graciousness.

So beautiful, he mused sleepily. Really so very lovely, with those improbable violet eyes.

The way she gazed up at him, so wistfully. "My angel," she had called him. Then she had been silent again, so silent and still.

Get your copy of *While You Were Dreaming* from Amazon, Barnes & Noble, and other major booksellers!

All Books by Celeste Bradley

Debut Novel

Fallen

The Liar's Club

The Pretender
The Impostor
The Spy
The Charmer
The Rogue
Wedding Knight
(a Liar's Club novella)

The Royal Four

To Wed A Scandalous Spy
Surrender To A Wicked Spy
One Night With A Spy
Seducing The Spy

The Heiress Brides

Desperately Seeking A Duke
The Duke Next Door
Duke Most Wanted

The Runaway Brides

Devil In My Bed
Rogue In My Arms
Scoundrel In My Dreams

The Wicked Worthingtons

When She Said I Do
And Then Comes Marriage
With This Ring
I Thee Wed
Wedded Bliss
On Bended Knee

The Courtesans

(with Susan Donovan)
Unbound
Breathless

The Haven Holiday Series

Sleepless in Staffordshire
While You Were Dreaming

The Vixens of Vauxhall Series

A Liar Under the Mistletoe
(a Liar's Club holiday novella)

&)CR

For more information about Celeste's books,
visit: CelesteBradley.com

For updates on upcoming books and events
by Celeste Bradley, you can join
The Voice of Society newsletter
and be the first in the know!

Reviews

"When it comes to crafting fairy tale- like, wonderfully escapist historicals, Bradley is unrivaled, and the second addition to her Runaway Brides trilogy cleverly blends madcap adventure and sexy romance."
—Booklist

Desperately Seeking a Duke (*Heiress Brides Book 1*)
"A humorous romp of marriage mayhem that's a love-and-laughter treat, tinged with heated sensuality and tenderness. [A] winning combination."
—RT Book Reviews

"A tale of lies and treachery where true love overcomes all."
—Romance Junkie

The Duke Next Door (*Heiress Brides Book 2*)
"This spectacular, fast-paced, sexy romance will have you in laughter and tears. With delightful characters seeking love and a title, [this] heartfelt romance will make readers sigh with pleasure."
— RT Book Reviews

"Not only fun and sexy but relentlessly pulls at the heartstrings. Ms. Bradley has set the bar quite high with this one!"
—Romance Readers Connection

Duke Most Wanted (*Heiress Brides Book 3*)
"Passionate and utterly memorable. Witty dialogue and fantastic imagery round out a novel that is a must-have for any Celeste Bradley fan."
—Romance Junkies

"A marvelous, delightful, emotional conclusion to Bradley's trilogy. Readers have been eagerly waiting to see what happens next, and they've also been anticipating a nonstop, beautifully crafted story, which Bradley delivers in spades."
—RT Book Reviews

About the Author

Photo © Charles M. Fitch 2014

CELESTE BRADLEY is the *New York Times* bestselling author of more than 24 Regency historical romances, including the extremely popular *Liar's Club* spy series and the *Wicked Worthingtons*. She has twice been nominated for the RITA Award by the Romance Writers of America. Before becoming a writer in 1999, Celeste was an artist who specialized in pottery and ceramic sculpture. Although originally from the South, Celeste now resides in New Mexico. "It is one of the last habitats of the Free Range Human." She is fond of food that someone else cooks, animals of all sorts, painting, drawing, reading, and grandbabies.

Manufactured by Amazon.ca
Bolton, ON